GW00507756

Hornets' Nest

Edyr Augusto

First published in 2007 by Aflame Books
2 The Green
Laverstock
Wiltshire
SP1 1QS
United Kingdom
www.aflamebooks.com
e-mail: info@aflamebooks.com

© Edyr Augusto Proença, 2004

English translation copyright © 2007 Richard Bartlett

First published by Boitempo Editorial in Portuguese as *Casa de Caba*.
This translation is published by arrangement with
Dr Ray-Güde Mertin Literarische Agentur, Bad Homburg, Germany

ISBN: 0-9552339-84
ISBN-13: 978-0-9552339-82

Cover design by Ludwig Wagner, www.zuluspice.com

Printed by Guangzhou Hengyuan Printing Co, China

Hornets' Nest

Edyr Augusto

Translated by Richard Bartlett

Fireworks. 23h40. Nazareth Heritage Complex. Mr Guedes receives the order from the festival director to light the fireworks. And so it has been for seven years, ever since he arrived from Marapanim and got the job. He followed others who had gone before him. While the crowd rumbles, nervous, impatient, he heads for the army barracks where, on the football field, the great mass of fireworks is set up. A few assistants are already running to take care of the fireworks set up in the Basílica, most of them at the famous fountain and the courtyard of Our Lady of Nazareth church.

Three men are in a Golf which comes along Braz de Aguiar street, makes a right into Generalissimo Deodoro and parks in front of a video store, shut. They jump out and head to the NHC.

On the acoustic shell stage, the band Sayonara ends its set. The crowd can't bear to wait any longer. They've eaten, they've drunk, they've flirted, they've sung and now they're pushing. Gangs of kids add to the usual confusion. Guards push through with youngsters brutally handcuffed.

On the 12th floor of the Queen Vesper building, the Pastri family also waits anxiously for the fireworks. From up there, the view of the Basílica is magnificent, illuminated, the colourful crowd, the frisson which feeds on itself, the infernal racket, intense heat generated by the jostling bodies.

Valdomiro Cardoso is already seated at one of the small tables put out by the bars during the festivities. Even though he is alone, he has been well looked after. Getúlio, the owner of the bar, knows he is a good customer. He asked for his first bottle of Cerpinha beer with the certainty that he would be there until daybreak, with energy enough to accompany, with tears in his eyes, the Círio pilgrimage's candle-lit procession, following the replica of the Blessed Virgin Mary back to Gentil Bittencourt college.

23h55. Mr Guedes meets his assistants, some smelling strongly of alcohol, which has never been a problem as they always behave correctly and spend the day working hard.

7

Walter Vasconcellos is night porter at the Queen Vesper building. He sways with the festival. He accompanied the Círio. The people of Pará can guarantee the biggest pilgrimage in the world, with one and a half million people on the streets. On the second Sunday of October, they carry the figurine of the saint, from the Sé Cathedral (to where it had been moved in the Festival of Transference the night before) to the Basílica. He likes the movement. The girls passing by. The domestic workers, released, who are constantly coming and going. Now he is alone. Everyone knows that the firework spectacle is about to begin. He stands in front of the doorway and also waits expectantly. Even in the fairground the queues are motionless. Whoever is on the big-wheel must have a brilliant view, he thinks. All eyes turn to the Basílica. But three men arrive and push him inside. They bolt the door. They get into the lift on the ground floor and press the button for the 12th floor.

The Pastri family are all at the window, curious. Maria, the mother, is on the telephone. Dondinha, the housekeeper, is the most animated.

23h57. The decorative lights on the Basílica are switched off. Mr Guedes gives the order and the fireworks begin with a deafening roar.

The three men use a master key and enter apartment 1201. Silently, cautiously. Dondinha is the first to realise something is happening. In the midst of the fireworks and the crowd's screams of pleasure, six people are murdered by large calibre shots. Seeing the rockets, bouquet of colours, roman candles and fountains illuminating the sky, the crowd goes ah! In the apartment, Dondinha receives the first shot, in the neck, falls and lies groaning, not moving, not being able to do anything while, without much resistance, but terrified, the rest are killed in an unhurried act, precise, professional, passionless. Maria receives a shot and lets the telephone fall. The last thing she sees is the porter, at the entrance to the room, in a pool of blood. The apartment is illuminated by the fireworks that slice through the sky, and the crowd down below, ah! On leaving, coup de grace. Father and mother, two children, the housekeeper and the doorman, Walter Vasconcellos.

00h05. Valdomiro Cardoso is already on his second Cerpinha. He looks the girls up and down and calls out to them, but none of them shows any interest. All of them look skywards, at the fireworks. In the air, the smell of gunpowder and smoke. Three men pass through determinedly, one of them bumps into the edge of the metal table, but does not apologise. He thinks of objecting, but leaves it at that. He merely looks at them to assess the extent of any likely uproar. There are three of them. He turns back to his beer and notices something on the ground, and his memory immediately recalls the rapid passage of that object, falling from some part of one of those three men, at the moment of impact. It's a keyring. Fuck it. Imbecile. Annoyed, he looks at the keyring, old, from some car spares shop in Castanhal. He reaches into the gutter. Fuck it. The three men arrive in silence at the Golf. Mr Guedes declares his work with the fireworks to be over. He makes the sign of the cross. The year is not yet over.

Golf. The three arrive at the car in silence. As they open the doors, two men appear and order them to get in. The show their guns. The three obey. One takes the steering wheel, another the passenger seat. Two motorbikes, alongside, escort them. The motorcyclist calls on his cell phone and confirms something with someone. They head for Gentil, in convoy. Listen, man, these guys are clean.

Be cool that they're clean. The guns. Pass those pieces here. Okay. The job's already done, I know. The boss ordered us to take you to a safe house where you can lie low.

That's not what was arranged. Those are my orders. He'll get in touch. Pass by there. Damn, I don't like surprises. Be cool. Up yours. Yours too.

The convoy leaves Gentil, opening a path. Takes José Bonifácio. Almirante Barroso.

We have to stop there at the bus terminus. Later. Not now.

Highway BR 316. In Ananindeua, they turn right. Aurá. Che Guevara informal settlement. Everyone asleep as they pass through. In the middle of the jungle. The car stops. The motorcyclists dismount. Without being ordered. Silencers on the ends of the barrels. They put their hands through the windows and shoot without emotion. A bullet in the forehead of each one. The one sitting in the passenger seat turns and also fires, just to make sure. Calmly they take out two bodies, still warm, still twitching and put them in the front seats, one as driver, the other as passenger. They pour petrol over the bodies. In the car. Set it alight. Watch, from afar. They get back on the motorbikes and head off. One of them on the cell phone. Everything's sorted, boss.

Referee. His eyes are still red from crying and from a whole night without sleep. He accompanied the pilgrimage and stayed, as always, hanging on the railing at the Gentil Bittencourt college, awaiting the entrance of the Blessed Virgin. Now he goes back down Nazareth street, following that route out of habit and also to breathe the clean air of the bright morning. It's a public holiday until midday, although many people take advantage of it to take a break until the Tuesday. Valdomiro thinks of his bed and the good sleep he will have. Not due in at work until the following day, an old arrangement made with his boss, in the accountants' office where he has worked for many years as a messenger. One pint at Garrafão and then finally home, on Trinidad Square. It's an old bungalow, which gives the impression of being in need of attention. But that is external, and a first impression. Valdomiro lives alone. In the house where he has always lived. An only child, his parents died, and he remained in the house. Quiet, introspective, preferred scapegoat of his colleagues at the office, he has revealed himself as a football referee. Yes, really. He never made it to the classic games and now his time is past, but it's adequate as a pastime. Blowing the whistle in the rough and ready night games of the Pará Town League, at the Pará Club, and over the weekends, in the suburbs, on the dirt fields where the youngsters who work hard from Monday to Friday participate with everything they've got. And there Valdomiro reigns with authority, controlling tensions, taking decisions which cause disgrace and ecstasy in equal measures. When he puts on his impeccable uniform, Valdomiro is no longer the quiet messenger, circumspect and abused, but a respectable football referee, for those 90 minutes like a king, even with the Pará Town League. Businessmen, doctors, public functionaries of the highest order, all bow to him, all line up to receive the yellow card, red card or a warning. And in the majority of cases they receive them with a certain pride, as if in confirmation of their fantasy of being football players, forgetting their status, their financial power. Sometimes it's a game between teenagers, and his authority needs to be exercised in a harsher manner. He has already been threatened, but no-one has ever lifted a hand in his direction. In the role of referee he is another person. That short little man, rotund, with his cabbage legs, is transformed into a giant. But when it all ends and they, whether players for the Pará Town League or team members of the Crematorium, go to a beery celebration after the game, he is once again the messenger. He goes straight home, to his castle where a whole world awaits him.

Behind that apparently poorly maintained façade there is a clean house, painted, secured, with a few alarms, in which he moves naturally because he has moulded everything to his requirements. Trinidad Square always has problems with thieves. But not here, and rightly so, he is always prepared for any attempt. A loaded revolver, cleaned from time to time, ready to go into action, kept in the drawer of his bedside table. Ah, that day has yet to come. He goes to the fridge, pours a good glass of cold water. Takes off his clothes, sweaty and with the smell of the people. Empties the pockets. Notices the keyring. Thinks it would go well in his collection, obsession he has had since childhood, when he collected Revell models, matchboxes, bottle tops and keyrings. After a bath, he falls into bed. He is not in the mood to take a look at his video or record collection. It is time to sleep. Little monkey pleased with a keyring, he thinks, already on the edge of sleep.

He awakes at about three in the afternoon. There in his bunker only the watch shows the passage of time. It could be any time at all. He is hungry. He places an order with LigPizza. The champion of junk foods. Alone. He is relaxed. He could call Edwina, but not today. Leave it for tomorrow. She will organise a good young chick to dispel his lethargy. He looks at his video collection. It has been a while since he watched *La Dolce Vita* by Fellini. Yes. He also has Buñuel, Antonioni and others. It is quite unusual for a messenger from an accountants' office who lives on Trinidad Square to have a video collection of the cinema's most sophisticated directors. No it isn't. It is his expertise. His father retired as a salesman travelling the interior of the country. Life was passing by and he did not wish to pursue his studies. Quiet, very quiet. He never missed an art session on Fridays at the Palácio cinema. There he came into contact with the great directors. He pays no rent, never in arrears with his rates and taxes, low usage of lights, transport vouchers, meal vouchers, junk food and a little money for incidentals. Valdomiro lives for himself, and the rest can go to hell. He has no wife, nor wishes for one. The presence of his mother was far too overpowering for that. He took care of her until she shut her eyes out of pure old age. She was always right. Spoke only when she was certain. Quiet ones gain the most. She exercised her authority at the right moment. He found employment at the accountants' office which had passed from father to son, and there he remained, always correct, discreet. Now he not only has confidence, but authority. With no skill at playing football, they were ordered about by that man dressed in black who made them more skillful, and those of greater ability stood down at his orders and decisions. His mother was still alive when he qualified and bought his first uniform. If he never went to whistle at the famous Remo or Paissandu grounds it was because he didn't want to. He quickly came to understand that the game is held together by those out of the limelight and that it actually becomes a battle as soon as the two teams come on to the field. So as not to damage his impartiality, he remained on the outside. He was also aware of the possibility of having his name printed in the newspapers. His name, his activities, interviews, none of this was important. On the contrary. Life was passing by and he remained a loner. With the death of his mother, he gradually transformed the house into a bunker. Television, video machine, CD player, videos, records, collections. Life, there outside.

The pizza arrived. He ate to the closing scenes of *La Dolce Vita*.

He wandered through the house and saw the keyring again. It was time to put it in his collection, look at the old things again, the most beautiful or valuable. There were two keys, one ordinary and the other, K19, obviously from a locker at the Hildegardo Nunes bus terminus. He knows because, on refereeing a game in Salinas, he left a spare uniform in one of those same lockers, then, on returning, he went directly to Matinha where he refereed another game. Instantly the memory of the encounter came back, the three men passing by, quickly, huddled together. He had thrown the keyring into the gutter, but then he went back for it, for his collection. He was bursting with curiosity. He was curious, he for whom nothing out there was interesting if it wasn't CDs with movie soundtracks, videos and refereeing. There was nothing for it. He got dressed, called a taxi and went to the bus terminus.

E-mail. It was time to read his e-mails. He looked to one side and saw Pat sleeping, exhausted, satisfied. He covered her naked body with a sheet. He went to the bathroom and had a shower. Wrapped in a towel, he went to the office in the apartment facing Central Park. Opened the laptop, connected and began receiving messages. One. Turned pale. Read it again. Thought for a few moments. Replied that he was on his way. Asked where she was. The time had come. He got dressed. Picked up some cash. Filled a suitcase with clothes. Left. At the entrance hall he dispensed with the services of the bodyguards. He called a taxi. Went to JFK airport. Managed to get a flight to Miami. From there, to Rio de Janeiro. He ended up in Belém. The driver wanted to take him to the Hilton, but he asked for the Hotel Central, more discreet. In his room, he called, but no-one answered. He hung up. He would begin his search the following day.

He woke up early, went for a walk. Rediscovering the city. The mangroves. The people on the streets. Where could his sister be? No-one else could know about his return. She was in hiding. He tried to remember friends in common. Three years away had made a difference. Sufficient time for her to put her plan into action. He had not expected it, but his life had also changed a lot, in an abrupt fashion. Where could Isabela be? He went back to the Central. He sat for a while in an armchair, with the treetops of President Vargas in front of him. Only then did he ask that they bring the newspapers for the past three days.

He recalled Pat and everything that he had left behind. Damn. There were matters to be put in order and, more than anything, save Isabela. He could have stayed in New York, in luxury, safe and sound. But no. Now he had no idea of what lay ahead. Isabela had gone all the way. He would help her. And Pat was in the past. A good past. A rock star. Global star. Here, he didn't know, but in the United States and in Europe, a great success. And he, as her boyfriend, was part of that. Meetings with record company executives, actors. Acquaintance with other stars. Big names dipped into their pocket to obtain favours. It wasn't important. Not even the drugs which were offered on trays. He really liked it, and she too, from the look of things. His nom de guerre was Fred Pastri. Discreet, he managed to survive the curiosity of the press. And it was purely by accident. He was on holiday in New York. He was walking in Central Park and Pat crashed into him on her bike. Hurt his leg. She took him to her apartment and called her doctor. There, everything began. She was already a success in the city, ready to launch her second and explosive album. From there onwards, the world opened for Pat Harrison, a beautiful blonde, with pert breasts, born in Nashville, but who always knew what she wanted – and it had nothing to do with country music. At 17 years old, she ran away from home with her boyfriend, became a go-go girl in the Big Apple. She took part in auditions for singers, became part of a band which played in bars in Soho and was noticed by a producer. A bet that came good. A strong temperament, a proud nose, but who encountered in Fred the partner she needed. The silent type, discreet, faithful. He told her almost nothing about his life in Brazil. In the Amazon. His record was clean, she assured the music company. It was his way, that's all. Pat had finished the last show of a long tour. They returned to the hotel. Made love. She was still reasonably drunk, from being on stage. She slept. He went to read his e-mails. Now he was here. There was a knock at the door. The newspapers.

Agony. Where am I going to fit, Netinho thought, squashed, on the back seat of the Golf. Killing had been part of his life for a long time. Always to order. Without involvement. Carried out with precision and professionalism. Efficient. A service. He had obeyed and received. For the rest of the time he worked in a motor spares shop in Castanhal. He sat there, leaning back. A few days earlier, that girl had come to look for him at the back door. He had known Isabela since they were children. They had grown up together. The Pastri family was rich and powerful. I don't know what happened. If they changed. Just as he began to be interested in girls and could even ask them out on a date. And now she appears, asking him to look after all those papers. Asking him to not even open it to have a look. Just look after it. Trusting. He was the only one. She needed him. Can't say no. How, if she had never left his head? During all those years when I had disappeared, I never had a girlfriend. First, because it was dangerous. Second, because of Isabela. She said the papers were a matter of life and death. That I should look after them. She would come back to fetch them. Then we could talk.

I didn't open it. Out of respect. Who knew what she was up to? The boss called and gave an order. He as well as Taílson and Do Carmo. Those two were from Thailand. He knew them. They had already done jobs before. They received the address and instructions, details, of the timetable. An idea came to him. He asked to stay in Belém a few days longer. Perhaps he would bump into Isabela, who knows? Okay. It's up to you. You won't do anything stupid, hey? Obviously. Don't even think about it.

That Sunday, they arrived in Belém as night was drawing in. Give me a few minutes at the Terminus? I need to leave a change of clothing so I can spend a few days here, holed up with a chick. Damn, Netinho, you're a real fucker, man. You've got chicks everywhere we turn. Imagine all those kids...

He hired a locker and left the old bag, with clothes and that envelope. Yes, he had travelled with it. Wasn't it a question of life or death? Who knows, women things. They would talk. It could be good. Life could be good. He fastened the locker key on to his keyring. They went into the apartment and opened fire. He wavered when he realised, but it was a job and not the time to be asking questions. The biggest doubt was the reason for Isabela's absence. That is what he was thinking, there, squashed on the back seat of the Golf, escorted by two motorcyclists from the Military Police. The driver and the other were also military. He recognised their mannerisms. So, was everything okay or messed up? Do Carmo bristled, but that guy said some man would pick us up and take us to a safe house. To stay out of sight. Could it be? There's never been betrayal, can't start now. What to do? Car moving, unarmed. He looked at the terminus when they passed by. Better to say nothing. At times like these silence is worth gold. Were they returning to Castanhal? No. This here is Aurá. Informal settlement. He looked at the others out of the corner of his eye. We need to do something. Wait until they stop before reacting. Who knows. Anything. Don't be nervous. Breathe calmly. You need to be cool. Watch everything. There's no time. There's a gun in his face, it's fired. He moved. He was wounded, ear ripped off. He remained motionless. Paralysed. And the others? The others? He senses the smell of petrol. Damn! Come on, move! Get out! Scream! Son-of-a-bitch, it's fire! He felt his flesh burning. A moment of clarity.

Castanhal. It was a Sunday during a rainy March, but there was some sun. Alfredo and Maria Pastri decided to take the children Alfredo and Isabela to the sawmill for an outing and to swim in the river. Business was doing well. There was plenty of mahogany. Or, rather, it came by river and, after being cut, was dispatched in trucks. They were next to the mill, having a swim and eating prawns, when a white VW Voyage drove up. It was Wlamir Turvel's car. Alfredo was not happy. It was Sunday, not a day to be doing business. He didn't like Wlamir, mysterious. Always involved in shady things. He went over to the car, to send him away. Tomorrow.

Maria was watching. Saw when the voices changed tone. Wlamir held out a paper. Alfredo said no. Two other men got out of the Voyage. She got up and went over to offer support. Before she got there, Wlamir punched Alfredo. He tried to react. The two other men began to beat him. She got there. Was grabbed. Wlamir, with the paper in his hand, asked that Alfredo sign it. They continued beating him. He was already disoriented. They kicked him in the back. She tried to protect him. In the struggle her bikini came loose. Wlamir had an idea. She struggled, but he took her, in front of her husband. Alfredo was tied up, unable to defend himself. Turvel stopped. Doing his trousers up, he held out the paper for him to sign. Pastri asked that he not kill anyone. Then sign. He signed. Now go because I am the owner of Rio Fresco sawmill. You have a house in Belém. Don't ever come back here. I'll do this to the two children. Maria remembered. She saw. Alfredo and Isabela were paralysed, in shock. She put on her bikini, picked up her beach sarong at the mill and ran to them. She tried to help her husband up, but he couldn't walk. She dragged him to the old Kombi. They went past their house only to pick up what was necessary. They picked up Dondinha who had stayed behind. They left everything. They went to Belém. Directly to the Belém hospital. It was an accident, they said. A problem with the spine. A hard fall. Perhaps he'll walk again. No-one knows. Castanhal, never again.

Alfredo was walking again. A little. A few steps. Lots of physiotherapy. No more work due to disability. He had something in the bank. Maria didn't know it, but she was pregnant. Twins. Daniella and Marcella. With all that suffering, they were born perfect. Maria sewed for people. She had many clients. It was enough to pay for the flat, the water, light and telephone accounts and some clothes. The children in public schools. They survived. Alfredo never spoke. The blow was hard. The humiliation. Impotence in the face of everything. The children who were watching. The children. They began to smile. Little smiles. Fred and Isabela are apparently normal children. They seem to have forgotten the trauma. They are studious, but in that apartment facing the Nazareth Heritage Complex where life had stopped and only the days passed by, the twins were growing up.

Wlamir Turvel. I was born already damned. My father, never saw him. My mother abandoned me to the nuns because she needed to earn her living standing on street corners. But today the old woman is doing very well. I give her everything she needs. That's what good sons do. I knew I would have to fight for everything I wanted. Nothing comes free. I was already working at 12 years old, swindling, cheating old women, earning my own. I learnt to live. I killed to live. I don't even have First Grade, but I know more than any other rich brat out there. Later, I bought school books. I was going to need it, I knew. In this world, you have to know people's weak spots. That's all. The rest comes easily. I wasn't born to be poor. I've done this and that, bits and pieces. I got cash together. I've already got people behind me. I gave a gift to the mayor. I know things about him. Clown. Let him shit in his pants. I looked at the City Hall and knew that one day I would be there. They spoke to me about demand for marijuana. So that's how it happened. I planted it, or sent for it. Belém consumed everything. I needed space. The Rio Fresco mill, perhaps. Alfredo is a scab. I spoke with the local magistrate. I had him in my pocket because of a shipment of teak. That guy was no fool. He drew up documents transferring ownership of the mill to me. One Sunday I went to his house. He was at the mill, swimming in the river. He never made it easy. Took a beating. I fucked his wife. Beautiful woman. When I saw those breasts out of the bikini, I couldn't help myself. Not like that. I think he was completely gone by then. But he signed. I could have killed him, but that would cause problems. The Pastris were well-known. They left, terrified. If you return, you die. Never again.

Now it's cocaine. It's better. Brings in more. I have the sawmill. Trucks. Boats. Money is no problem. The dream now is to get power. Conducted a campaign and was elected mayor. Brilliant.

Now I had even more freedom to conduct my business. I wanted more power. Huge business. Was elected to state parliament. I quickly learnt the political game. Perhaps I was born learning. I wanted to be governor. With him, now, Antonio Jamelotti, my right hand man, diligent student of the bureaucratic machinery, since being mayor of Castanhal. His accomplice in business. He was born to serve. One day, who knows, he could be his successor. That way, he will always be comfortably in power, and contented. It was a difficult election. But he has lawyers, actors, police, judges, councillors, parliamentarians in his pocket. The Workers' Party candidate almost won. It was necessary to bribe many people. He spent more than he had intended. But now he was governor of Pará. He forgot to mention his wife, Cilene. She was a secretary in a construction company in Belém. He liked her. He thought she would be another easy fuck. She wasn't. She held firm. Helped in his roles. She also wanted power. They climbed the ladder together. She always knew she wouldn't be accepted in polite society. She was common. Spoke wrong. Dressed badly. And so? They all came to eat out of the hand of the powerful. Now they are to be found, in bed, ready for sleep. Each one on their own side. But partners. She knows everything. It was her insurance. Now a re-election is coming. There will be difficulties, once again. The country is going through a wave of decency. Some associates in Rio de Janeiro have been imprisoned. The Colombians are using his route more and more. With this, the danger grows. The business involves drug trafficking, cargo theft, illegal sale of wood, money laundering, robbery, executions and bribery. Lots of bribery. Now he travels by helicopter. More efficient. Between one city and another, stop over at the sawmill. Created a house to relax in. Being alone. Thinking. The flights have been frequent. Thankfully, the press have been pacified with the tons of official propaganda. He is drawing up plans with Jamelotti when he receives an envelope, sealed, confidential. He opens it. He gasps for breath.

Locker K-19. In the taxi, Valdomiro Cardoso passed by the Basílica and recalled the passage of Our Lady of Nazareth. Now, over for another year. The driver commented on the mess left by the pilgrims. Tomorrow it'll be clean again, he said, looking at the big wheel in the park and remembering his times as a child. He got off at Hildegardo Nunes bus terminus. Goes directly to the lockers. Cautiously, looking around, no-one seems to be interested in him. He put the key in, opened, and, at the back, found a bag, one of those travelling bags, well used. When he went to pay he said he had lost the receipt. It was cheap. It must have been left yesterday, last night. Keeping his curiosity in check, he took another taxi and headed for Harbour station. Few people. Fewer tourists. I wonder how this place keeps itself going, he thought. He stayed outside, making the most of the end of the afternoon, high tide, pleasant breeze. He sat at one of the tables at Capone. He waited for the waiter to serve him and withdraw. He opened the bag. He found a simple change of clothing, of cheap material, and an envelope, unaddressed. And now? He wasn't certain. He should have left everything where it was. Been honest. He shouldn't have gone meddling. Thankfully, there was no money or documents. But what about this envelope? To open it or not?

There was a letter, handwritten, one sheet. And another envelope. Inside, various newspaper clippings. Photographs of documents. A few notes. He read.

Netinho, read this carefully. What you are going to see below might seem shocking, even weird for you who has led a quiet life in Castanhal. In the past couple of years, you have no idea, I have been there a few times, and looked for you. I know you work at OK Autospares, but those times you weren't there and we couldn't talk. What follows is the value of my life and the purpose that I have decided to give to it. You might think it strange, so long afterwards and with no contact, putting these papers into your hands, but it's just that I need to trust in someone and I chose you. You remembered our friendship, since college. We had to leave Castanhal in a hurry and I continued my life in Belém, but I never forgot about you, someone for whom I felt a great deal. I believe that you felt the same. We didn't have time to develop that. I still feel the same. I am at an important moment in my life. Many things could happen, good and bad. It could be that everything turns out right and I come back here to ask for all this back and will finally be able to lead a normal life and begin our friendship again. If it doesn't turn out right, I am going to need you for an apparently straightforward job, but of great importance to me. It's easy. If it turns out right, I will appear in your shop. If not, I want you to hand this envelope over to a journalist, Orlando Saraiva. The address you can find in any newspaper stand where they sell the newspaper he edits. It's easy. You don't have to identify yourself. Better if you don't. Just hand it over. So easy and so important. Pray that everything goes well for me. I am counting on your friendship.

Isabela Pastri.

Valdomiro also knew who this Orlando Saraiva was, the 'Orlando Urubu', crusading journalist, feared by politicians and criminals, prevented from publishing his stories in the bigger newspapers, for fear of upsetting the biggest advertiser, the government. Because of this he decided, with the help of some secret friends, to publish his own newspaper, always sold out but which no-one ever admits to reading. He could hand it all over. But wouldn't it be more honest to return this bag, so that this Netinho can make the handover? Yes, I could do that, but first, please forgive me everyone, I am going to read what is written there.

Family murdered at NHC. An entire family has been shot dead in an audacious crime which took place in a building located in the Nazareth Heritage Complex. The preliminary findings of the police indicate that the perpetrators of this crime committed the act on Sunday night, during the festivities which closed off Nazarene Square. Alfredo Pastri, retired, his wife Maria and their twins Daniela and Marcella, in addition to the housemaid Maria das Dores and the building's doorman Walter Vasconcellos, were shot dead with large calibre bullets. The bodies were found following an alert from a neighbour, who sensed a bad smell coming from the apartment. Apparently the perpetrators forced the doorman to take them to the 12th floor of the Queen Vesper building, where the slaughter took place. According to residents, who did not wish to be named, the family was amiable, and Maria, who was a seamstress, received clients at her home. The doorman was well trusted and had worked in the area for more than five years. Also, according to the residents, there are two surviving children who were not at the home at the time, a son who lives abroad and a daughter, Isabela, whose whereabouts are unknown. Detective Gláucio Lima, who is in charge of the case, said that his investigation was in progress and he could not say anything more. Access to the apartment has been restricted to allow the police forensic services to search for fingerprints and other clues. The Pastri family, according to the doorman who works during the day, was originally from Castanhal, but had been living in Belém for many years.

Fred was shaking when he finished and had confirmed details by reading other newspapers. He did not notice another report, about the discovery of the carcass of a burnt-out Golf, with three burnt bodies, at Che Guevara informal settlement, possibly related to drug trafficking. He cried. He recalled the events clearly, so long ago. He felt angry at himself for not having been with his sister. Then he felt angry with her for not having forgotten and for blundering ahead, even without him. Now, his whole family had been murdered. His sisters had nothing to do with this. And what had Isabela done to cause this slaughter? The past, the blood flowing, everything was beginning to collapse around him, he who had been in the comfort of an apartment facing Central Park only a few hours before. He needed to find Isabela and decide to press on or to run away, to disappear. He had some money put away in the United States. He could take his sister there. He could organise a green card and they could forget everything. Begin a new life, far from the shame. And to press on, would that be the right thing to do? That man had killed all the family, and you, coward, you want to run away, save your skin? One way or the other, he had to find Isabela. She should have been killed. She had escaped, I don't know how. But the risk she ran had not disappeared. He went to his laptop to open his e-mails.

Sauna *privée*. Carlito knew the owners. They owed him favours. He could use the sauna whenever he wanted. On Monday, for example, specially for him and his friends. He said that, as an artist, his Sunday was on Mondays. He worked all weekend, as a promoter in gay bars, where he did sporadic cross-dressing numbers, and pimped girls for the bosses. He had a book, noting the meeting, and received a percentage. Discretion was his greatest asset. He knew that it was the soul of business. He had his contacts, now and again he would travel inland and bring girls. He gave them shopping malls, education, learning. Some of them even managed to get married. Others went back. Others disappeared. They wanted to spread their wings. Fuck them. They became street whores. During that time of all the hookers the only one who was truly different was Sílvia, if that was her real name. She never gave her address. She seemed middle class, intelligent, educated. She said she liked money. But they all say that. I had to teach her a lot of things. She was a virgin. I didn't believe it, but it was true. A cherry that was sold for a great deal. And she was ambitious. Take me to the bosses. I want the richest ones. Don't you have politicians? They're the best. They pay their dues. But after a meeting with Jamelotti she disappeared. She didn't even answer her cell, the bitch, ungrateful. I bet she's sucking the cocks of all those white-bellies and raking it in. She should pay me what she owes. If she hadn't been on my books she would be a worthless whore.

He was with Dudu and Esteves, who had brought a boy to entertain him, one of those who seemed a bit out of it, pretended not to know anything, but can really perform when the time comes. That Esteves likes to pretend she knows nothing, understands nothing, stupid, stupid, stupid, I thought. The attendant switches on the sauna and goes back to the reception. Discreet, him. Damn, shit, aren't you two going to leave me in peace here in the sauna? I also want to relax, boneheads! They leave. Completely naked. The boy hiding his cock, becoming embarrassed. What's your name? Dioclécio. What? Dioclécio? Fuck, what sort of screwed up name is that? It sounds like some sort of disinfectant. So far away, man, sitting there like you're frightened… I leave you with those queers… Don't you want to come closer?

The door of the sauna was open. The attendant, with a frightened expression. Behind him, a man in black. Revolver at the attendant's back. Who's Carlito? No-one spoke. Who is Carlito, dammit! The bastards looked at me. The whole world imploded. Come here, you, shit faggot. Come here, dammit! What have I done? Don't you know. The pistol whip catches him between temple and nose, grazing, cutting and hurting. I didn't do anything! I'm just some poor bastard! Another pistol whipping. What have I done? Again, I'm only going to ask you once, okay? Only once. Where can I find Isabela Pastri? Who? Kick in the face. Kick in the back. I'm going to give you a chance. I think it's your last one. Who is Isabela Pastri? I swear that I don't know. I've never heard that name. Isabela? For God's sake, if I knew I would tell you so that you stop hitting me. Motherfucker, my patience is finished! Shot in the knee. A hole. Intense pain. He starts screaming, crying and groaning. Kick in the knee. The others beg, scream, plead to not do any more. Carlito, for the love of God, tell him quickly who this Isabela is. In the desperate plea, a mistaken interpretation, as if he really knew who she was. You tricked me, you worm? No, I swear. I don't know. I don't know and I can't make it up because I don't know who she is. Damn, you're making things much more difficult. Don't you like living? Do you want to live? Then talk, bonehead. Talk before your time runs out. One shot and Esteves falls with a bullet in the head. I'm going to ask you again. Where can I find Isabela Pastri? One shot kills Dioclécio. Bullet in the back of the head. The attendant says everyone must just stay calm. A shot in the head. Dudu begins shitting all over the place. Putrid stench in that ambience of steam and heat. Talk, worm! Tell him because I want to live! Your friend is scared, faggot. It's up to you. Are you going to talk? Listen sir, I swear that I don't know her. I've never pimped any whore with that name. I've no girlfriend called Isabela. Okay. A shot in Dudu. The rest of the magazine into Carlito. He left. Closed everything. Got on his motorbike. Headed off, stopped and called. Boss, nothing doing. That faggot really didn't know. Yes, I did the job. All clean. Waiting for your instructions. Yes sir. See you later.

Isabela Pastri. I never forgot. On the contrary. Every day of my life I remember it. Fred and me. At the mill with mom and dad. Those men came. They hit him. Raped her. As I write I see those scenes over and over again in slow motion. I will never forget that face. That man. We ran away to Belém. I stayed silent a long while. There was nothing to be said. Gradually things returned to normal. Normal? It was never normal. Nor with Fred, in his own way. My father never really walked again. Nor worked. Nor left home. The new home. That apartment in Nazareth. The day-to-day sadness. Always. Day after day. Mom made friends in the square out front. She began to sew. Dondinha with us. I grew up, seeing people, and the memory ever more vivid. I wanted to know the reason. My parents said nothing. Dondinha was forced to, one day. She said the name of that man. Wlamir Turvel. My father had a sawmill in Castanhal. There were illegal shipments. My father was caught in the act. He was squeezed. There was disagreement over the price. My father was stubborn. He dug his heels in. Turvel had a judge friend. He drew up a deed of sale. Forced my father to sign. The old man took it, but said no. He changed his mind when my mother was raped. We lost everything. The sawmill was what we had. And the apartment which was an investment. And disability benefits. And mom's sewing. No-one to turn to. The two of them had come from the interior of Paraná. Without family. Lovers. They got married in Castanhal. Father sold the truck. Bought the land at the mill. And the twins? Are they children of father or of Turvel's rape? That was never explained. It was part of the tragedy. Of my vengeance. Mine. Only mine. Fred's, also. Two against the world. But his head is more in the clouds. Mine is weighed down with hatred. My life is not like that of others. My life is my vengeance. That's what keeps me going. Alive. And, with every piece of news about Wlamir Turvel, I am revitalised. Each victory. Each election. Each photo. News. I read, cut it out and keep it, hidden away. I showed it to Fred. We were teenagers. We went to school and returned home. To that environment suspended in time. Only mom's clients bringing any vibrancy. No parties. No pastimes. Dondinha tried to drag her off. Mom didn't have time. The sewing and the twins. Papa. When Wlamir Turvel appeared on the television, he changed the channel. No comment. Fred went to university first, to study administration. The following year I went, to study social work. It wasn't a waste of time. Everything was a preparation for revenge. I saw Luciano. My boyfriend. A great guy. I know he liked me. A lot. I didn't. But I felt affection. Would I be able to experience affection at least? He took me to the cinema, theatre, walks. He never took me home. Those were my boundaries. Fred too, with the daughter of an American preacher, Eve, porcelain white, pretty, nice. She also had to struggle. He gave in. She thought him the very silent type. Men's brains are different. He signed up for the army. Learnt to use firearms. That would be useful. Our plan was not ready, not yet. James, Eve's brother, went to the United States, during his holidays. He wanted Fred to go with him. With what money? The preacher helped out. The ticket, bought from that side, is much cheaper. He was walking in Central Park, in New York. He was knocked over by a bicycle. The girl took him to her apartment to clean him up. She told James that he could not come back with him. He had to stay there. It seems the girl is somewhat famous. She is a rock singer. Known around the world. My world is my revenge. Forget Fred. Now it is up to me. Wlamir Turvel was elected governor of the state. Incredible, but true. Father of the people, he called himself. He thought the sky was the limit. He was getting ever further away from me. How would I reach him to get my revenge? A little longer and he would be in Brasília, the capital. Dear sweet Luciano gave me an idea. He told me he had met a friend who had become a call-girl. She worked for some Carlito, one of those gays who pimps chicks. Who service even government ministers. That gave me an idea. To kill Turvel, quite simply, was much closer. He must suffer. Lose all hope. Fall in the dirt. And then die. He had to suffer. To pay for all that he had done to my family. To lose everything. Dear sweet Luciano. I told him that I had to do some research for university, to do with call-girls. I asked him the name and phone number of his friend. And then I disappeared. Simply disappeared. He was an honest sort. He assumed he had hooked up with a normal girl. That was not the case with me.

I phoned Fátima, Fafá, and set up a meeting. She was an attractive woman, young, well dressed, but with a sensual manner. She told me she earned well, that she even had a rented apartment. Her photos were in Carlito's book, which he took to his clients. Luciano told me that you're studying at the university. No. That's what Luciano thinks. But it's not true. I want to be like you. Introduce me to Carlito.

Carlito, this is the chick I told you about. She has already chosen her *nom de guerre*, Sílvia. And she has something I didn't tell you about but you're going to like to hear. She's a virgin. Unfucked. Cherry intact. Not so, Sílvia? It's true. You can do any test you like. Didn't I tell you? She's a gold mine.

You're a virgin? I don't believe it. At your age? How old are you, 23, 24? Imagine that, these days they lose their cherry even at nine years old. A virgin at your age. Sorry, yeah, but it's difficult to believe. Okay. You really want to be a hooker? Do you know how it works? You know you have to pay me commission? Do you have a place to stay? You know you can get called at any hour. Have you got a phone? You need to buy a cell phone. Let me buy you one. You can pay me back later. Take off your clothes. Yes, every little bit. Come on, little one, I don't have all day for this! Move your hand, dammit. Let me see. Look, love, for me, its like examining a prize bull, okay? Hmmm… so, Fafá, this girl's got it all, d'you know that? Tits, arse…that hair… where have you been hiding? Let me put my finger here… hold on, keep calm.. Hey! Girl! A virgin at your age? You're at university? You do know that you're going to miss lots of classes? You've made your mind up already, haven't you? Fafá, you brought her here. She's your responsibility, okay? I'll send you a cheque later. Have you got some time? So we can start lessons right now. Fafá, get Caco on the line for me. Yes, that sexy hunk. He's damn expensive, but well worth the money. Get him to come here.

The guy arrived. Attractive, after all. Carlito took us to his room. Told Fafá to come in as well. He explained to Caco that I was a virgin. That he wanted to teach me a few things. I took off my clothes again. Caco also. I understood that I actually had to learn, if I was to succeed in my revenge. And it was that which gave me the audacity I needed. I noted, in his eyes, admiration for my body. Carlito, Caco and Fafá were telling me what to do. How to appear enamoured, available. How to feign sensuality, affection, desire. To sing praises. To caress. To take the hands of men on my body. To take hold of them. There, in that place. To have patience. To recognise size and thickness where there weren't any. On that afternoon I learnt to be a whore. Caco was excited. Not I. I took it all very seriously.

And if the man wants to fuck my arse? My girl, your first response is no. But a no like someone who is afraid of the size of his cock, understand? Something which makes him proud and carries him forward. The cost increases, you understand, hm? I'll teach you. And if he wants to come in your mouth? It's yes, girl, just like that. They like it. Makes them feel strong. Costs more. You're liking this, aren't you, Caco? Such a hard cock... She is very beautiful, really, but she's not for your prick, okay? She's a gold mine. Go. You can go. You too, Fafá. Thanks. The cheque is on its way. And you, what's your name? Ah, Sílvia. Let's talk. I came from nothing. A worm who the whole world screwed. But today I've got a name. I've got credibility. Today, no-one screws with me, you understand me? Some have already tried and were fucked. One phone call by me to the chief of police and that person is fucked, thanks to me. They're all my clients. You understand me? You're a virgin. I'm going to sell your cherry for a lot of money, okay? They call wanting to know if there's fresh meat. They ask if I've got virgins. They like that. I'm going to sell your cherry. I'm going to call them. Take this phone here. I'll let you know.

Carlito, make it expensive. I want men in the government. You know who likes it. I want ministers and higher, okay? If I'm going to give it, let it be expensive. I'll get rich, and you too. Don't worry, nobody knows me. I hardly ever leave the house.

You want to start at the top, hey? Okay, I admire someone with ambition. Without it I also wouldn't have got anywhere. Minister? Higher than minister, only the governor, my darling. You, hmm?

Whore. Fafá was waiting downstairs. We went to the shopping centre to buy clothes. Hooker's clothes. Gang designer jeans to squeeze and lift the arse. Low-cut blouses. High-heeled shoes. To the salon. Bikini wax. Eyebrows. Hair. Make-up. I learnt.

Luciano doesn't need to know about this, okay? Must never know.

Girl, be cool. Watch where you're going. I know. I also know. Don't worry. Thanks. I won't forget your help. I'll pay you back with the first money I get. I know. You're honest. You could even get discovered that way. All of a sudden, they have a party in some or other place, it happens once in a while, and they see you. We're in this together. You're very beautiful. You get me? That night she thought of sending Fred an e-mail, telling him everything. But, then, she decided to keep quiet. Let him get on with his life. Make the most of life. He likes his girlfriend. He has a right to escape. Me, no. No-one at home liked her new appearance. The colour of her hair. She gave some excuse. In her room she took the time to look at her collection of clippings about Wlamir Turvel and his achievements. She smiled. Finally, it was beginning, pay-back, her great motivation. Vengeance. She looked at herself in the mirror. A new face. The bikini wax had left her with little pubic hair. Fafá had said that's the way it should be, really. That it would be better with the sexy panties she had bought. Okay, now came the waiting. Two, three days. A Saturday morning, the cell phone rang. She was woken up. She cut the noise off by answering. Carlito.

We're in luck. We're going to earn lots of money. The men are crazy for you, girl! New pussy on the block, they're crying out, the shits. You ready? It's costing him a lot. A very lot. You're now going to start giving it good. It's the Minister of Culture. Saulo Miso. A shit. Thinks he's intellectual. Intellectual of shit. Full of himself. There's some who say its enough to finger fuck to get him to come.

He likes fresh pussy. Listen up. He's going to fetch you at three in the afternoon, there at Harbour Boulevard. I said you'd be in jeans and a white blouse, low-cut. Your hair's blonde? Fafá told me. He's 55 years old, or thereabouts. Greyish, beard. He's going to ask you for Carlito. You tell him that he's been set up with you. That's the signal. Do what he wants. Make him enjoy it. He's paying in cash. None of this chasing of cheques. Moan, scream, make him feel as if he's powerful. He's going to check his condom to see if there's any blood. To confirm. If he enjoys it, he'll call on you again. He'll mention it to the other ministers. Afterwards come straight here. I want my money. I want you to tell me everything. Agreed?

I was not so clueless, nor so inexperienced after all. These days, no-one is. There's films, magazines. There've been nights out on serious dates with Luciano. Though under control, she fondled his penis and knew exactly what she was doing. But now everything was about to begin. Everything for which she had been preparing for her entire life. There was no space for sentimentality. She got dressed and looked at herself in the mirror. She was no longer Isabela Pastri. Externally. Internally, Isabela, ready for revenge.

The man with the tired face and a slight curl to his lips said the agreed words. She responded. He took her in his car, with tinted windows. They went to a motel nearby, in Pedro Álvares Cabral. He ordered wine. Asked her name. Tried to be sophisticated. She played her role. Behaved like a frightened little lamb, inexperienced, but with great desire. Drank only enough wine to wet her lips. He undressed her. He approached her from behind and used his hands. Admired everything. She, actress, cold, but apparently excited. Yes, the KY before the encounter was essential. His fingers worked and were satisfied in finding the wet warmth between her legs. He left the lights on and got undressed. Hairy, flaccid belly and a normal penis. Nothing more. She feigned praise, to encourage him in facing the defenceless, virgin maiden. She held his member and made it hard. Put on the condom. Asked him to deflower her. He demanded that she scream for it. She screamed. That thrust hurt deeply. Very deeply. Tears welled up, but were discarded. She groaned as if she was satisfied. The encouragement led to quick enjoyment. When he withdrew from her he went straight for the glass of wine. She sang his praises. Said that it had been like a dream. He asked if she had experienced pain. She said that her desire had been so much greater. It was like a dream. I like older men. He asked if she recalled her father or something like that. She almost lost it. She said yes, but her father had died many years ago, when she was a child. Perhaps it could be his absence, he said. Perhaps, she agreed. Lying there, the used condom, like a sliver of blood. Proof of her deflowering. She praised him again. Told him that he had been the first. He responded that there would be many more times. He asked if she worked, studied. She said she had studied, before coming to Belém. She had come from Ananindeua recently. If you need anything, come and find me. I'm the Minister of Culture, did he tell you? No, I didn't know, she lied. She asked if he was powerful as Minister of Culture. After me there is only the governor. And you see that often the governor doesn't do anything without asking me. If you need anything, you can ask. Do you want it again, she heard herself asking and realised that vengeance had superseded any other emotion. She was prepared. He said no. One good blow is better than many. She said it would have been wonderful, nevertheless. He said that he knew that losing your virginity was a very important moment and that now she could relax. There would be other times. He went to get the money. She went to get dressed. He asked her to hold on. He touched her breasts, her arse, her pussy. You're beautiful, what was your name again? Sílvia. The money is there next to your purse. He would drop her off at Harbour Boulevard. Now, in the car, even on that short route, he seemed different, distant, cold, a stranger. She felt abandoned, like a sucked-out orange. Fuck it, she thought. It had begun. It hurt. It was humiliating. But the objective was noble. She told Carlito. Paid. He said that she should expect more phone calls. She was good merchandise. He had sold her for lots of money. The men are crazy for you, Sílvia! That night, in bed, she could cry to her heart's content.

The search. Eager, Fred opened his e-mail inbox. Message from Pat. *Darling, what's happened? Where are you? Please tell me something. What have I done? I love you, baby. I miss you. Please come back!* Another, from Isabela. It was brief. *Fred, they're killing us again. I'm asking you for help because I'm scared. Please tell me where you are. I'm at a friend Fafá's house, on Chaco Travessa. It's a new building, but I think I'm going to have to leave here. It's very dangerous for her and she's got nothing to do with this matter. Anyhow, she'll tell you where I am. Isabela.* He checked when the e-mail had been sent. Monday, 23h20. It was late on Tuesday afternoon. He had to sleep after his rushed journey. He called for a taxi. The building was new. He didn't know it. The doorman said Fafá was not there. There was some suspicion in his gaze. He asked about his sister. He didn't know her. Miss Fátima's friend is Miss Sílvia, but I haven't seen her at all today. I've been here since seven this morning. And this Sílvia? There's nobody up there now. He left the phone number of his hotel, asking him to call if Fafá returned. Then he decided, with a heavy heart, to go to the coroner's office to see the bodies. Identify them. He went to the fridges. He lost control. Trembled, asked for a glass of water, cried. There were his loved ones, having suffered so much and with such a cruel fate. He signed the papers. Someone would inform him of the funeral. He waited and they came. He accompanied them to the chapel. The burial would be on the following day, at eight in the morning. He sat down to spend the night in vigil. A man entered the chapel. He didn't notice it. He was lost in his own thoughts. He felt hatred, humiliation, fear, revolt all at the same time. Anger at himself for living with no worries, far from there, while his parents were murdered, his sister was almost certainly on the run and being hunted down. And now, in Belém, his hands tied, without knowing what to do. And fear. Was he a coward?

Alfredo Pastri Jnr? Good evening, my name is Orlando Saraiva, journalist. I know perfectly well that now is not an ideal moment, but I would like to talk with you. Obviously it does not have to be right now, we can set some other time. It's just that they informed me at the coroner's office of your arrival and I came here.

Look, I expect you understand my situation. My entire family has been murdered. As soon as I heard, I came immediately. I live outside Brazil, so I don't know anything. I don't know of any reason for this to happen. We have no enemies. My parents were quiet and kept to themselves. So, apart from my grief, I have absolutely nothing to say to you. Please, good-bye. Mr Pastri, I beg your pardon once again. But, apart from yourself, there is another survivor, your sister? Where is she? Abroad also?

Yes, she's abroad. She may not be able to arrive in time for the burial. Now, if you don't mind…

The journalist left. He could not say anything. Nor did he know what to do. Perhaps go and find Luciano. Could he still be manager at that cinema? The night was long, humid and sad. The cemetery was alongside the BR 316 highway, and he only heard, in the distance, the drone of traffic. He dozed off. The sun and the noise woke him. The funeral took place. Apart from him, the padre and the undertakers, two men in coats and ties joined them. When it was all over, he made to leave. He was in a bad mood with grief and exhaustion from a poorly slept night. The two men came up to him.

Mr Pastri Jnr, I am Detective Gláucio Lima and this is Inspector Pereira. I am leading the investigation into the tragedy of your family.

Mr Lima, I am very tired, I spent the night here in mourning.

I do understand. Please, answer just a few questions and we can talk at length later on. Do you live outside Brazil?

Yes, I've been gone about three years now, living in the United States, in New York. And, before you ask me, I can guarantee that my parents had no enemies. My father was pensioned off due to incapacity, an accident many years ago. My mother was a seamstress, dressmaker. Both kept very much to themselves, my father never left the house.

Besides yourself, sir, there is also your sister Isabela, who is not in the area at this moment, not so? Could you tell us where she is?

No, sir. I believe she is travelling and should arrive at any moment. I too do not know where she is, because she didn't tell me.

Have you had any contact with your parents, with your sister Isabela?

Now and again. I called sometimes, on birthdays, but we got on well. I came here to introduce the woman I'm living with in the

United States. My parents were well-meaning. Now, if you don't mind. One thing, Mr Lima, I would like to visit the apartment. Could I?

Pereira, call Dagoberto and tell him that Alfredo Pastri Jnr will be coming there. You understand that the apartment is sealed for investigation by the police forensic team. Detective Dagoberto is there and will accompany you on your visit. I should inform you that until it has been released, you can't take anything from there, okay? Where can I contact you, Mr Pastri, later on, to talk?

I'm staying at the Hotel Central, there on President Vargas.

Thank you very much. My condolences. Farewell.

He was tired. Very tired. With a wounded soul. But he decided to go to the apartment at that very moment. He had to see everything. Find some lead. Isabela was in trouble. Detective Dagoberto was waiting at the reception. They went up. On entering, he smelt the strong chemical cleaning products. Yes, the bodies were in a state of decomposition when they were found. He saw chalk outlines where they had fallen. Events harden people. He walked through that place where he had spent a large part of his life, understanding, finally, that that oppressive environment, sad, was like the preamble to an impending tragedy. And that life had taken him to New York and, nevertheless, everything was linked to that Sunday, at the sawmill, in Castanhal. Everything. He, Isabela, Dondinha, his parents and even the twins themselves, were in eternal doubt as to whether they had been conceived before the rape or not. He walked through the entrance hall. Went into the lounge. Outside, NHC square lived its day-to-day life, with students, children, the elderly and lovers. Went to his parents' bedroom. Sat on the bed. Looked at the photos on the bedside table. Lingered. Waited until Dagoberto relaxed on a sofa in the lounge. Went to Isabela's room, straight to the box of clippings hidden in the wardrobe. He hid them in his shirt and trousers. No-one could know. He wanted to know what had happened during the time when he was absent. There they were, in the photo, him, her and the twins, with Dondinha. What a pity. He sighed deeply and went back to the lounge. I want to be sure that you didn't interfere with anything, not so, Sir? Rest assured. I'll come back when it is released. Why not. Can we go?

He went to the Olímpia cinema, to look for Luciano. The boy said that he had gone out, but would be coming back. And there Luciano came walking in. He seemed just the same. A few kilos more, perhaps. He received the emotional condolences. I was shocked. You know that Isabela never took me there to get to know her family. But the news hit me hard. Where is she? Do you know? I came to ask you if you know anything. She sent me an e-mail asking for help. Something has happened. I don't know where to find her. If I knew… She kept very much to herself. She had no friends. The last time I saw her was when… Did she end it with you? Long time back. You were saying. I was telling her about a friend who was a call-girl. She said she needed to interview this girl, for some project at university. Then I never saw her again. It's as if she's disappeared off the face of the earth. Fred, I still like her. I haven't got married, have on-off relationships. You can count on me for anything. Despite the circumstances, it's been a pleasure talking to you. He went back to the hotel. If he had known that they were so close… In his room, he re-read the clippings which he already knew and put aside the more recent ones, taking note of Wlamir Turvel's deeds. His election, his police disputes, his alliances. The launch of his candidacy for re-election to the government of the state of Pará. Whatever it was that Isabela had done to this man, it had provoked great hatred, great fear, for him to react so violently. He had abandoned all scruples. Killing an entire family. Could that be what happened here? He feels so powerful that, when in a corner, he abandoned all caution? That's to say, she must be well hidden. Only Isabela can resolve this. Where am I going to find her? He linked up his laptop and sent an e-mail to Pat. *Pat. Sorry. I don't know if I'll come back. I have things to do. One day, maybe, I'll tell you. Love you forever. Fred.*

Rage. Motherfucker! Cunt! Whore! Bitch! Bollocks! Jamelotti, look at this. Do you see what the motherfucking whore has done to me? Look closely. See these photocopies. And more, see this Xerox from the laboratory. See? Now read this receipt. Do you see? Cunt, that one, wanting to blackmail me. A pile of shit. A family of traitors. Shit! She deceived me, that's for sure, she deceived me. Should we deceive her as well, Jamelotti? Hmm?

Of course, Wlamir. She deceived us all. As God is my witness, and now? Get over there, they're not going to lose faith in me. We're fucked. Fucked and badly paid. That woman is throwing shit into the fan. And the re-election? And the businesses? It'll go down with your reputation. Fucking bitch!

I'll end up a right prick. She's going to die. Die for the insolence of deceiving me. Die because I will not be held accountable to any of them. That's what a person gets for being considerate. She wants revenge, but not with me. Jamelotti, do you have her address? Find it in the phonebook. The Pastri family. Yes, Pastri… yes, sir, so many years later. Have them killed. All of them. I don't want to know. Cut the evil from the root. You know what to do. You don't need to bring me into it. Careful, Wlamir, you might start something! Let me worry about that. Get it done. Today. Now. Finish this story. Call me. I want to know immediately. And then get rid of all the tracks.

Antonio Jamelotti knew what to do. Obviously this time he had to take greater care. He called Lobato at OK Autospares in Castanhal. I want Netinho. He'll be in charge. Get those two from Thailand, understand? Okay. The chief is pissed off. This is a serious job. Discreet. Important. Payment for each head. Double. That's it. Double. The plan is as follows. The address is in that building, there at the NHC. The NHC, in front of the Basílica. Okay? Good, Sunday is the end of the Círio, the pilgrimage, that stuff. They go at sunset. Wait for the fireworks. You know, the fireworks, at midnight. The whole world will be watching the fireworks. They can go up and do the job. Then they come back, straight back, on the same route. I'll send the money like the other times. Look, Lobato, this is serious stuff. Ugly stuff. Professional job. Don't drop me on this. I know. I know. I trust you. The boss as well. I've got people to check who'll call me to say if everything's done. Relax. Go with God.

He called Colonel Silva. Silva, come here, to see me. I'm at City Hall.

Silva, you've been with us for a long time. Done well, gaining power. Gaining money, not so, Silva? That's true. I've got a job. Serious stuff. To be done by you and someone you can trust. A matter of life or death. Request from the boss. The boss. The governor. Your governor. Can I rely on you? A crime is going to take place. This Sunday. At NHC. No, no-one will find out. It's in an apartment in the building that's on the square, on the other side, you know it? Of course. There are three men. They're going to commit this crime and they'll run away. They'll be in a Golf. Everything is arranged. They'll park there on Generalissimo, just after Braz de Aguiar. When they get back to the car, take them for a ride and make them vanish. Vanish. I don't want anything left over. Not of the car, nor of them, got it? Take discreet men with you, that you can trust. Do you understand? Call me when everything is sorted. No, call me when they're with you and then, again, when you've sorted it. I'll explain it to you again.

Alone in his office, on that Saturday afternoon, he put aside the papers that had to be signed and the calls that had to be made. He smoked another cigarette, from the four packs that he smoked every day. And he thought. That fucking whore. And I liked her. Hot chick. I gave her everything she needed. She travelled with me. That's why it's said that men are led astray by a little pussy. He who was so skilled at managing his dishonest activities, never leaving tracks, and still duelling in the political arena, although he thought that fundamentally they were all the same thing, the fight for power, let himself be deceived by a girl. A whore. A Pastri. I should have killed them all. He remembered, vaguely, Alfredo's wife, whom he raped. She enjoyed it, she enjoyed it, deep down, she enjoyed it, he consoled himself. But now he was going to do what he should have done a long time ago. With a violence that no-one would expect. His secret. A monster in defence of his interests. No hesitation in killing. First I wanted money. Then I wanted power. Now I can own anything. But that fucking bitch, that Isabela Pastri, not bloody Sílvia. And she even called me Mimi, Little Mimi… Fucking bitch. What a person doesn't do for a bit of pussy. But the truth is that if one doesn't act with speed and precision, things can get complicated. She's got everything in her hands. The copies of those documents and that test. You mean to say that although he's old, Wlamir is still virile? A child. Cilene couldn't have children. But don't think about that any more. A child. And soon, by the look of things. That fucking bitch wants to pin me in a corner. Have her killed and it's done with.

He spent Sunday next to the swimming pool, drinking with Jamelotti. He guaranteed that everything would be done that night. He explained the plan and he liked it. Jamelotti knew what to do. Like a clone that follows orders. Cilene was at the house in Salinas. He sees she's taken her personal bodyguard, hand-picked. To fuck to her heart's content. Her life's her own. I don't give a shit. Each to their own. So, Jamelotti, you mean to say that little whore slipped through our legs, hey? You were the first, weren't you? No. The first was Saulo. Saulo? That retard who everyone thinks is gay? Then I fucked her. With all due respect, Wlamir, she is beautiful, truly. Sílvia. When you saw her, you ordered the world around you to leave. She was yours. She liked it. Or appeared to like it. The fucking bitch really deceived us. Now she's going to pay for it. I've already told you the story about the Pastri family, no? Alright. The fucking bitch came to get revenge. And you saw the test results? It's true, my friend, this old man doesn't shoot blanks. Old goat, hmm? Did you bring those papers to sign? I want to watch the game on TV.

Wlamir. The job's been done. Relax. Neat and tidy. It was Lobato's people. But there's one thing. I sent Silva, the colonel, to make them vanish. He's already called. It's all done. But there's a problem. Silva's people went there to confirm things. One's missing. Her. She wasn't there. Motherfucker. The bitch ran away, she sensed it, I'm telling you. Of course, you know there were no leaks. She found out, I know her. And now?

Damn, shit! At least we eliminated the family. At least that's something. That's to say the job was clean. I'm going to talk to Antonio José, to order it filed away and there we go. But we need to eliminate the bitch. Look, I remember now that gay who pimped her. By the name of Carlito. He arranges services for people. For me. For Saulo. For Antonio José. He arranges the girls. It's him who brought her. He'll tell us where she is. Eliminate him as well? Eliminate him.

Doubts. Valdomiro Cardoso returned home. He had a bath, went to the table, opened the envelope, read and looked through everything. The photographed documents, notes, photos in which the governor appeared in various places, with other people whom he did not recognise and the results of a laboratory test saying it was positive, pregnancy test, in the name of Isabela Pastri. Another note, for Wlamir Turvel. While he was reading, Valdomiro was getting tense, worried, even sweating. When he got to the end, he breathed deeply, looked once again at the photos of the notes and receipts, of the governor, spread out on the table and thought for a long while. He was scared. What he had in his hands was highly explosive material. Exposed, it could cause problems. Big problems. Bringing an end to his view of the world, discreet, his personal world. His security. This was enough to have someone killed. And if they had seen him taking the bag? My God, how could I be such an idiot, going to the Harbour Station! He thought of all his alarms and the burglar bars on the house. And that Isabela, where had she gone? What if she's dead? Would they have the guts to do that? Had she run away? He hadn't read anything in the newspapers. He didn't read newspapers. He had been looking forward to watching *Un Chien Andalou*, on video, but he couldn't bring himself to do so. In bed, with the light off, he tossed and turned, not sleeping. When he arrived at work he went straight to the newspapers. "Family Murdered at NHC". He read. The name Pastri. It was not Isabela. But those faces which bumped into me... the keyring... Son-of-a-bitch. I'm fucked. He hid his nervousness. He continued reading, passing to the sports section, looking for the results of the neighbourhood championship and the Pará Town League in which he had been the referee. Nothing had any importance any longer. For the rest of the day, instead of working, he thought of seeking out Orlando Urubu. He did not know him personally. He could be someone who doesn't hesitate to reveal his sources and, damn, his life would be in danger. He had an atomic bomb in his hands. He went to a magazine stand. There was the Urubu newspaper. He was nervous just paging through the newspaper and looking for Orlando's address, imagining himself the focus of thousands of eyes. There it was. He memorised it. He never forgot a phone number. He would keep it forever, well hidden. Or burn it. His life would continue as normal. His conscience worked overtime thinking of that murdered family. The home of that Isabela. Of the crimes documented in that envelope. He felt like a coward, leaving things as they were. Hiding away those revelations. He phoned. A woman with the voice of a maid answered. He's not here. He's coming back later. He decided to leave his number. His first name. It was urgent. A matter of life or death. He can call, no matter how late. He felt relieved and brave at the same time. Like when facing all the anger of a team when awarding a penalty against them, or a red card, obviously a poor comparison. Just that sense of justice. He put cheese rolls in the oven for dinner. Switched on the television just for the company. Today there would be no films nor listening to CDs. Nervous, he walked back and forth, waiting for the phone call. It was already past 11 at night when the phone rang, frightening him. For a moment he hesitated in answering it. And what if it was them. Them, who? Who knows. He answered. It was Orlando Urubu. He explained that he had found an envelope, in the street, and, opening it, had read important facts which should be made available to the public, explosive enough to send the governor of the state himself to prison. He had to repeat it, patiently, until he received some acknowledgement on the part of Urubu. It's just that many people call and sometimes it's pure rubbish. Where are you? Can I come there. No, actually, I'm afraid. Let's do this – do you know where the Albatross is? That bar there on the corner of Nazareth and Dr Morais? There. I think it's still open. There's always a few barflies hanging around. Are you a long way away? Half an hour? Okay.

Now there was no turning back. He would plead, an exchange of the information, which was excellent, in return for forgetting all about him. He could not be involved. It would be the end of him. When he arrived, Urubu was already there. I came quickly. I've had a busy day. Haven't even changed clothes. First the murder of some gays in a sauna, then I went to talk with a member of the family which was killed there at the NHC, did you read about that? I did. That's what I wanted to talk to you about. But first, I need to say something. This is the envelope. But I am only going to hand it over to you if I have complete certainty that I'm not going to be mentioned. In any way at all. You must forget that you've ever met me. That you spoke to me. That you received this envelope from me. Can I be sure of that? You won't be, in some way, forced to reveal my name? Not even by the courts? Look, Valdomiro, in my position as a journalist I can guarantee confidentiality regarding my sources. I don't know exactly what it is, but unless you have involvement in this matter, something that incriminates you, that reveals you as participant in some offence, you can rest assured. I understand your desire for anonymity. These days, things have become very dangerous. What one wants most is to be behind doors at home. That's it, that's it, behind doors at home. I'm just a simple messenger, in an accounting office. At weekends I'm a referee, imagine, football referee in local and league games. I found this left in the street. I think the colour of the keyring, something, caught my attention. I got it home and when I read it, I wasn't only reminded of you, of your fight, of the newspaper which you write, because, also, there were clear instructions that everything should be handed over to you. But I was afraid, you know how it is. Okay, it's this here, isn't it? You want me to open it right here? No. Please. Not here. Are you sure you left everything in there that you found? You've left nothing behind? Absolutely. I read it, was frightened to death and decided to call. That being the case, I can guarantee your confidentiality. I'm going to take it with me. I'll read it at home, as soon as I get there. Thank you very much. It's been a pleasure. Will you pay for these drinks? Leave it to me. Look, almost nobody has my phone number, but if you need to call ... Okay, look, I'll write it on the side, as referee. That way, if someone gets it, they won't know who it is. That's good. I can relax.

Valdomiro returned home relieved. Truth be told, he knew that, having seen what was in the envelope, it should not be opened there, at the Albatross, he knew. But he would very much have liked to debate the matter with Urubu. He knew about things. Knew people. Made connections. He would know everything. Who knows, soon he might build up courage and call, like, "how's things going?" Who knows.

Orlando called Edwina. Love, today's not going to work. I've had a terrible day and now I'm on my way home with work to be done. What? You read it in the papers. Look, tomorrow I'm spending the day here. I might have a great deal tell you about, and all of a sudden you're busy with something. Kiss, kiss. Ciao.

He arrived home, had a bath, and while eating dinner, with the TV on, searching for some news, opened the envelope. First he read the note from Isabela to Netinho. Then he saw some photographs. He rubbed his head. Read the letter. The first lines, skipped to the end to see the signature: Isabela Pastri. Pastri? The murdered family. She was not among the dead. Travelling, like her brother said? My God! This is going to rock Pará to its core. He looked at the photos and drew the connections between the people. Saw the documents. Notes. And that positive pregnancy test. Isabela Pastri? But some or other Sílvia is Wlamir's mistress... Yes, changed name. Revenge. Miss Vengeance. And now? Something's going on. It could, perhaps, be the greatest story of his entire career. He also thought that he might have gone beyond all his capabilities and could be in real danger. He re-read and re-examined everything. He was thinking of what he could do first. This was a real hornets' nest.

I arrived. On the spur of the moment, Fred Pastri decided to surf the internet for a while. When he got to the *Billboard* site, his first surprise. "Rock singer goes to Amazon." What? He clicked to find out more. "The rock singer Pat Harrison has left today for Brazil. She is going to discover the Amazon for herself. Pat has gone to meet her boyfriend, the Brazilian Fred Pastri, who travelled ahead of her. Assured of being accompanied by a press entourage, she said she would take the opportunity to highlight the beauties of the great Amazon rainforest." Brilliant. When is all of this going to end?

A sequence of blows to the pit of his stomach. Non-stop. Repeatedly. Pat in Belém. How did she manage to find out? Damn dangerous! The international press here. This situation. It's going to be even more difficult trying to find Isabela's hiding place. He thought of not showing himself for a few days. She must be staying at the Hilton Hotel. I need some time. I don't know how much. Some time. He heard the sound of his laptop alerting him to the arrival of an e-mail. He checked. In her passable Portuguese. *Dearest Fred. I already know where you are. I am on my way there. You're not going to escape like that, so easily. I am ready to get to learn about the Amazon. Know your family. Who knows, we might come back married? I'm arriving, my love. Find me at the Hilton Hotel. Kisses. Pat.* In the *Rolling Stone*, "Pat goes to Amazon". In the *NME*, "Rock on Amazon". It was international news. There were moments of a weariness so extreme that there was no energy left to absorb anything. Think of nothing. Rationalise. The delayed sleep, strong emotions, one after the other. Eyes closed. Like a stone. Sleeping. But the world doesn't stop. Some don't sleep a wink. Others asleep forever.

Love. Pat Harrison was a practical woman. Courageous. She knew the value of ratcheting things up a notch. That was her life. Overcoming challenges. It was hard, realising that Fred had left just like that. They were in a perfect moment. Success, money, understanding. They had just finished an exceptional tour of Japan, of Europe and the United States. Now they were spending some time on holiday, composing new music, thinking of a new album. About six to eight months of peace and quiet. Escaping the mega-exposure of her image. She awoke relaxed, at about two in the afternoon. Head heavy from a deep sleep. Body tired from the gig. Tired from the long tour. All that remained were meetings in the office the following week, when the revenue would be accounted for and other business would be decided on. The record label wanted to launch a DVD and a CD of live recordings. She was resisting. It was too soon.

But we could make a good deal. She had the idea of developing her own label, with new artists. Now she had the investment for that. The crowds who went to her concerts and the shops to buy her work would guarantee support. Fred wasn't there. Perhaps he had gone for a walk in Central Park. After a long bath and breakfast, she allowed Martha, her assistant, to come in. Have you seen Fred? No. Fred hadn't come back. She noticed the absence of a few of his clothes and his laptop. She didn't understand. He had left his cell phone. Like someone cutting their links. She began to worry. Completely preoccupied. Martha busy with phone calls. Nothing. The housekeeper came to inform them that the night doorman had seen Fred leave with a suitcase. So he had gone then. Could it be another woman? I doubt it. I came from nothing, I know people. Returned to Brazil? No. He had said. We have no secrets. Okay, he didn't tell me everything about Brazil. The Amazon. What is the city really like? Belém. Pat is devastated. The deception added to the physical and mental tiredness. She makes a decision: to find Fred. I'm going after him. I don't care. Today I can do what I like. He must have had a good reason to do it. Martha, I need to find out. Call the record company, discreetly. It must come out in the press. I want to know where he has gone. Someone can check the airlines. The business of his passport. Go, Martha! Go to the computer. He must at least have left a note. Sent an e-mail. Nothing. So she sent one to him. *Come back, my love. What have I done to you?* So tired and unable to sleep. State of shock. Sad. She put everything aside. The DVDs with scenes from the concerts to select. Her guitar. She wanted Fred. The information arrived on Tuesday, at about midday. Fred was in the Amazon. Martha already knew what Pat would do. Let's go there. Handle the documents. Today. I'm going to pack. The studio will find out. What shall I tell them? Nothing. You can't do that. You're famous. I don't care. Okay. Say that I went to the Amazon, on holiday, to meet up with Fred, who went ahead. It'll fill the press. I can't do nothing. Suddenly, it would be alright. I want to get to Brazil today. Today? I don't think you can. I'm going to check the flights. Charter a small jet. I can. I will. It's important to me. She checked her e-mail inbox again. Nothing. Then she sent an e-mail saying that she was on her way. She left the apartment, with

Martha and two bodyguards. Call those guys. Just to find out. Martha called the press on her cell phone. At the airport, reporters. Nothing to declare. *Billboard*, *NME* and *Rolling Stone* are going to send journalists to accompany you. Good. Finally, on board, she slept.

It was dawn in Belém. The temperature was pleasant, but stifling, somehow. The local representative of the recording company was waiting for her. Martha dealt with him. Difficult. He didn't speak English. She went straight to the car. There's a Hilton Hotel here? Yes. Even the press have arrived, some time ago. Through the window, she observed a very different reality. Very green. When they got to President Vargas, it improved. The mangroves. She found everything beautiful. She went straight to the presidential suite. We're going to find Fred! But it's five in the morning. Alright. I'm going to check my e-mails. *I don't know if I'll come back. I have things to do. One day, maybe, I'll tell you...* What things? If he had said something, I'd have helped. Now he has money. He has power. What could it be that he hasn't told me? Those silences about his life in Belém... could it have been some crime? Fred's not like that. He's a peaceful man, considerate, discreet and loving. She ended up dozing off on the sofa in the suite.

Headway. Saulo Miso had already fucked her three times. More passionately each time. He explained himself. His wife worked in another office and they seldom spent time together. She was happy at work and had no time for him. To listen to him. Sílvia listened. His bravado, his small victories. Enough already. She told Carlito that she had had enough of the Minister of Culture. She wanted something more. Higher up. Chill, little one, your name is already doing the rounds in the cabinet. There's people calling me. Go home. I'll call you, you'll see. Aren't we doing good business? I'll look after you. When you came here, you looked like an altar boy. Now, a beautiful hooker, very tempting. It would be my luck that I don't like girls. No distractions at work. Carlito called. Now it was one Antonio Jamelotti? Camelotti? No, don't get it wrong, dammit, Jamelotti. Chief of Staff. He's a turd, but a powerful turd. Close to the governor. Joined at the hip. Like Cosmas and Damian. Enemies say they even share an arsehole. He's short and fat. Piggish, sweaty. He only likes young ones, but it was Saulo who told him about you. Look, if they don't tell each other you won't get lucky. You know that. He's going crazy to fuck you. High stakes. Fresh meat to be shared out. He's in the know about everything. Make him cry for more, darling. I'll give you a tip. Finger-fuck him. Finger fuck? Put your finger up his arse so that, as they say, he squirms. Up his arse? There are some who like it. You didn't know that. Saulo didn't ask for it. No. Jamelotti likes it. I don't know if he'll ask. When he's close to coming, put your hand closer there. If he lets you, put your finger in. I'll tell you where to go. To Harbour Boulevard? No. He's more discreet. At Castanheira shopping mall, because there's lots of movement and no-one will notice him. At Castanheira? He'll come from Augusto Montenegro. Straightforward. We agreed? Don't forget to bring me my cut. And tell me everything, darling.

It was Tuesday. The two of them, at the back. The driver, in front. Jamelotti had brought his own car. They took the BR 316. Close to Marituba, tarred road. He had ordered it tarred to make it easier for him to get there. If I put myself up for election one day, these shits will just have to vote for me. What was your name, then? Sílvia. You know that everyone at the office talks about you. Really? You're bloody beautiful, shit. Lift that dress up a bit more. Let me see those thighs. Delicious! It was a holiday home. The driver remained waiting outside. Large room, large bed, family photos on the walls and on the bedside table. He took off his clothes first. Sweaty. Fat. Flabby. His belly hung down, hiding his penis. He came to undress her himself, already panting. She did the whole bit. Showed she was aroused. Said that he was sexy, wonderful to touch. He lay on his back and asked her to get on top. She struggled to get his member, but managed. It was tiny. There were rolls of fat everywhere. Nausea. In the middle of the act he asked for time out. He got up, lit a cigarette. He was panting. He came back. She had to start the blowjob all over again. Now he lay on top of her, almost suffocating her. She was putting her hand closer. Yes, he let her. She put her fin-

ger in. Bang. He rolled his eyes and groaned in pleasure like an animal, mumbling sweet-nothings, slapping her, grabbing her neck,
leaving marks. He withdrew from her, sat on the edge of the bed,
panting. He lit a cigarette. Marvellous. Delicious. Heavenly. Son-of-
a-bitch. Jamelotti, fuck it. You're fucking good, no? A real treat. I'm
so sorry. Sorry, for what? I enjoyed it. I enjoyed it a lot. You know
that whores are here for your enjoyment. But I enjoyed it. Forgive
me. It's just that you're so gorgeous. You don't have anything to
apologise for, girl. You're brilliant. Man, what a thrill. Listen, that
inserting of... well, the finger there... in... well, that stays between
us, okay? Can I count on your discretion? Look, I'm very gener-
ous... You can count on me. I've already said, I enjoyed it. The
money is over there, all yours. I'm going to call you again. I want a
repeat performance. Spectacular. Let's see, hmm, Thursday, okay?
Call Carlito and set it up. It's great for me. I also like you, Sir. Ah,
not so formal, drop this Sir rubbish... I'm Tony to you, okay? Of
course, Tony. Jamelotti called to set up an appointment for
Thursday, and from then on, twice a week, they were in that place.
Carlito said that Jamelotti paid for exclusivity. Sílvia was for him
alone. Only him. What have you got in that pussy that these idiots
are so crazy for you, hmm? Can you imagine that even Souzinha,
the Minister of Agriculture, has called me because of you. I said you
had an exclusive arrangement. With State House. He confirmed it.
For them politics was more important than anything, the exchange
of favours.

Two months later, the itinerant government of Wlamir Turvel
was moving to Santarém. Jamelotti called and asked for her to go
with him. You know how it is, far from home, after a tiring day, having a lady waiting... Yes. The possibility of meeting Turvel was
increasing. She had to be very cautious. Her big moment was arriving. They travelled by air. She went straight to the hotel suite. She
spent the whole day waiting, watching TV and thinking about what
she would do. He arrived at sunset. There was a reception. She
asked to go with him. She wanted to see people. She could mingle
with other people. No-one would know her. Jamelotti was hesitant.
I don't want you talking to anyone. I'm paying, I have that right.
She lowered her eyes. He apologised for his thoughtlessness. You

know that I don't think of you as a prostitute. You know, it's been a long time since I felt such affection for someone like you. I know, I know, I'm not an idiot, it's a business arrangement. But I'm also made of flesh and blood, my dear, stressed from work. You make me happy. Listen to me. Perhaps you're only doing this as a professional, but what you're doing, you do so well. I'm not only doing this as a professional. I also like you, Tony. I've grown to like you. I don't have any false hopes because I'm just a hooker, but because of the exclusivity, I have grown to like you. Listen, my love, when we come back up to the room, we can talk about the two of us, okay? Did you bring clothes? Please, nothing too provocative nor a short skirt, no naked back. First, because I'll be crazy with jealousy. Also, because it's an official reception and the like. I'm going to have a bath and help the Gov. You'll get to see him at the reception. She had spent the whole time lying on the bed, wearing only her panties, moving, waiting, on remote control. She got up, gave him a kiss. He fondled her breasts. Later, later… He got in the bath. She could smile, satisfied. This could be her moment. She controlled her anxiety. She waited for him to leave and went to get ready.

When Sílvia entered that hall, there wasn't a single person who didn't undress her with their eyes. There were a few women, almost all much older, middle-aged, wives of the local politicians. Pretending to be shy, she mingled, but her eyes found the eyes of Wlamir Turvel. Circled by guests, he did not stop chatting to the avid audience, but his eyes accompanied her, fixed on her. She knew she had him hooked. Now it was a question of time. She picked up a passing glass of champagne. She stood in a corner, at the same time watching the throng and feeling herself watched by all those men. She had her hair tied up, subtle make-up, a black dress which emphasised her breasts, pert, and her back naked. Completely naked. She saw Turvel coming in her direction, but in a tortuous fashion, stopping at every group, smiling at every meaningless compliment, acknowledging good causes, considering requests in all earnestness, putting papers in his pockets, with Jamelotti by his side, who she knew was red, not from heat but from jealousy. They stood in a corner. They must be discussing some political matter.

Who is that woman? Wlamir, that woman is my woman. The girl I've been going out with for some time. Please. Do you think I haven't seen your eyes? That obvious? I'm sorry, but she is so damn beautiful. Where did you find that one? It's the same one Saulo spoke about that day. Saulo? Soyabean? Yes, Saulo Miso. Jamelotti, I want her. Wlamir, please, not her. I want her. No, Wlamir, not her. Don't do this. I'll buy her from you. Buy her? Think about it... You don't want me mentioning that fling of yours, there in the finance office? I know, you want to get some kickback. I know, you know that. Dammit, Wlamir, this is not worth it. Wlamir, I don't know. I like her. I like her more than money, than power, or than a hooker. Dammit, Wlamir, you're fucked in the head. Fuck off. Dammit. Motherfucker. Give it a rest, dammit. You're going too far. Ask for all the films from the photographers. I don't want any photo of her. No news, nothing. Get going.

It took great self-control to keep breathing and respond, seemingly only half interested, to Wlamir Turvel's greeting. The objective of an entire life, it was here, in front of her, *completely* interested. How's it going? Having a good time? It's certainly hot enough here in Santarém, isn't it? Jamelotti tells me that you're his guest here. I want to thank you for gracing us with your presence. Jamelotti is a good friend of mine. The person closest to me. I've asked him for something which only very close friends can agree to. I asked him to let you come with me tonight. Just like him, I also sometimes require a different kind of companion, feminine, intelligent, another type of conversation. The whole day spent on politics, business, and one is likely to become heartless. And the last thing I want to do is become heartless. Will you keep me company. Why not, Your Excellency, but you seem to be surrounded by friends. Friends? If they could, they would cut off my head. That's the world of politics for you. But I may need them one day, in fact. We can chat a bit later on, in my suite? I'll send for you. Please, stay with us. You are most beautiful. Your presence is enchanting.

I can't! I can't do anything! Jamelotti is like a pepper, bright red, panting, sweating, in the room, while Sílvia packs her bags. Tony, I don't want to go, Tony. I want to stay with you. Me too! I have plans for the two of us, but I can't do anything. He's the boss. He's the governor. When he orders, I obey. Do you always obey? Have you never disobeyed? You don't understand. It's not that simple. There's lots of other things involved. I don't want to go, Tony. My dear, let's do the following. Be crap with him. Do it with no passion. Oh, my God, how it pains me to say this. Do it badly. Do it so that he doesn't like it. Hey, perhaps, you'll come back to me. All that's left is for me to ask this of you. Don't be yourself, if that's at all possible. She cried. She wanted to laugh at that humiliated fatso, but he would certainly receive some compensation. Now, yes, they were cheating on each other. They came to fetch her. She entered that spacious suite, bathed in half-light. In its depths, seated, looking out the window, contemplative, smoking one of his almost 80 daily cigarettes, Wlamir Turvel was waiting, full of love to give.

Your Excellency… Sshhh. That word, excellency, is ugly coming from your mouth. It's you who ought to be called 'My Lady'. Like a queen. Call me Wlamir. It's much sweeter. Much gentler on the ear. I've been thinking, here in the darkness, how the beauty of a woman rises above anything in our world of politics and business. Many people don't think so. I do. Here we are, closing deals haggled over during a day of tough negotiations, and, suddenly, an angel enters this scene. It seemed as if everything became soft and gentle, you were floating on clouds, all eyes fixed, I think someone even tried to make a wisecrack, but I wouldn't allow it. The entrance of a queen. Something to be respected. And, now, you're here. My dear… Sílvia, your name is Sílvia, they tell me. Have you ever heard mention of the loneliness of power? You spend the entire day at the centre of attention and at the end of the day you're alone, in some hotel room, left with your thoughts. How fortunate that you arrived. Would you like a drink? Look, you should be banned from walking around in a skirt.. and slacks… banned from walking. You are so beautiful. You could cause accidents on the street. Are you from here in Pará state? I am. From Ananindeua. From Ananindeua? That's right, my parents came here a long time ago from Goiás… Ah, Goianas, I could tell from your features, the colour of your eyes, your skin. But I'm a true child of Pará. The beauty of Pará shines through, my dear. What do you do? I'm studying social work, at Universidade Federal do Pará. Very good.

Are you about to graduate? I haven't been there very long... I understand. Looking at you, I understand. Should we go to the room? We can talk in a more relaxed environment, in bed. It's late already and we're leaving very early. Do you smoke all the time, so much, like that? I smoke. It's my vice. Sometimes I think I was born with a cigarette in my hand. But I have strong lungs, I believe. Or, better, you'll see. The man, without clothes, lost all his formidable nature. His back was bent. Absence of a bum. Wrinkles. Folds of flesh, hanging. The smell of cigarette smoke impregnated everything. She had to control her nausea. No. She needed, now, at that moment, to conquer it. Defeat her inhibitions. Overcome her alarm signals. She had to use her most lethal weapon. When he turned round, she was already naked, seductive, arms spread wide. I'm all yours. Come. She outdid herself. She made love with her entire body. Gave herself over. Faked orgasms, rolled her eyes. He sucked violently on her breasts, anus and vagina. But didn't reach a climax. He tried again. He lit a cigarette. Head full of problems. She waited for him to unwind. She sucked him, passionately. That tiny penis represented everything. It was the possibility of success, and she took it into her mouth. His orgasm came powerfully, in spurts, almost hoarse groans, like someone releasing the whole day's problems and tension. She took it all. She looked at him, her mouth still full of sperm, and smiled, proud. Thank you. Excuse me a moment. She went to the bathroom, washed out her mouth and came back. To his side. Caressing him. Saying how he was appetising, handsome, powerful. And, gradually, licking his chest, his arm, his penis once again, first delicately, true professional, he saying that perhaps he wouldn't manage a second time, he wasn't as young as he once was, having to work, who knows with the cigarettes, he was hard, once again, and he was pleasuring himself with her. He got on top. He fucked her and devoured her. You're so beautiful! A goddess! Look at those breasts. Look at that arse. Beautiful! Are we going to come together? I'm waiting for you, yes? They came together. Another cigarette. What planet did you come from? That bastard Jamelotti, not telling anything to anyone. Girl, you're a real typhoon. It's been many years, such a long time for it to happen, no-one has made me so happy in bed. Beautiful! Stand up. Like that.

No, don't be shy. Stop that. You mean to tell me that a few minutes ago you were able to do all that, and now, in front of me, you behave like a little shy girl? Look at that beauty! Please, don't get dressed. Stay naked. Please. It's the most beautiful landscape I've ever seen. One moment. He called an official on the phone and explained that the aeroplane, the next day, was to be only for him and one other person. All the other ministers would have to travel in another plane. Listen, if... Wlamir, I must go back now to Mr Jamelotti, mustn't I? Back to him? Not on your life. Today you stay here, with me. Tomorrow we're travelling early to Belém. You're coming in my plane. That's okay with you? But, what about Ja... I've already spoken to him. Alright. Unless you want to go back... I'd be most upset, but... No. I don't want to go back.

It was just the two of them returning in the aeroplane. He tried to sleep, but she had his number, kissed him and, discreetly, unbuttoned his fly, massaging his penis. Girl, I'm not a young boy anymore... But you're so beautiful. Unbutton your blouse, please. Let me see, once more, your breasts... so beautiful. On disembarking, he asked for the cell phone of one of the drivers of the two official cars which were waiting at the airport and gave it to her. I'll call you. Keep it. She went back in the official car. She asked to be dropped off at Harbour Boulevard. She went back home. She threw Carlito's cell phone away. Her bet was placed. Now the wait for the phone call. The cards were on the table.

Fear. Be cool. It's coming to an end. Silva pitched up somewhere nearby, yesterday. An apartment there in the Marco district. Her friend as well, who owns the flat. There are some men keeping an eye on it. It was only her who arrived and that's it. Antonio José called me. I didn't recall that she had a brother. Same name as the father. Alfredo. Goes by Fred. Lives in the United States. Buried his family. The detective conducting the inquiry spoke with him. Gláucio Lima. That guy is clean, he knows nothing, doesn't understand. He's there in the centre. At Hotel Central, on President Vargas. I've already given the orders. Leave it with me.

You don't understand, Jamelotti? This could be the end of us. The opportunity that all those sons of bitches have been waiting for to nail us. And what am I going to do with the re-election? And if I lose the post? That bloody attorney-general shit, there in Brasília, is going to come down hard on people, for the kill. Get rid of that guy as well. And, motherfucker, find that woman. If she goes to the press it's the end of us. Suddenly some of those shits will want to stand up, give a great performance, and we're fucked. Call the heads of the broadcasters. Alert them that they could be fed a lie, a rumour, you know. No, don't do that. It could make it worse. Motherfucker. Son-of-a-bitch. I'll kill that woman. But first liquidate that Pastri that's still around. I've already cancelled everything today. I'm ready to deal with it. I'm going to send Cilene on a trip. Far away. As far as possible. She'll take the accounting records with her. Anything that comes back to me.

Cilene? Come here right now. I'll explain later. You need to go away. Far away, I don't know. I'll think about it. I'm going to have your bags packed. When you get back home, it's just for a change of clothes. I'll be there. I'm not shipping you off. Something serious has happened. It is, damn, serious, bugger, don't stress me so that I have an attack. Fucking serious. Don't you like your life? The money? The power? Then, dammit, get going. We'll speak here. I'm going to organise two trips. Get going.

Jamelotti? I spoke with Cilene. Have her take two flights. Switzerland. But first bring her here. The first flight. Wherever it's going. To the coast, to Brasília, direct to Suriname, who cares. Get it done. I want to take the tickets to the house. Just get it done. Any news? Shit.

Wlamir Turvel was scared. Little by little he understood the extent of the problem confronting him. He knew that Sílvia would be scared of handing everything over to the Justice Department. He had control over everything. Even the federal police. He had paid well to have such control. But the press was an unknown. He controlled it too, in exchange for a great deal of advertising. Now and again, close to re-election dates, there was provocative material. A game of cat and mouse. He knew. But suddenly, with that idiotic wave of decency sweeping the country, there could be some twit wanting the glory of toppling him. Knocking him. And if it was some little editor from one of those new ones, which have just started up, they'll snatch up the accusations, play them on the front page, the owner won't see it, shit in the fan. Motherfuckers. Too much stress. Now he lit another cigarette. He didn't have the courage to kill her himself. Could it be that he was in love with her? Was it really her? Who cheated on him? Who betrayed him? Who was now blackmailing him? But he wanted her dead. It was a vital necessity. It's her or me. Me. What a fool I was. She took him in completely. The cell rang. He saw on the screen. It was her. He trembled. Didn't answer it. Sat in the silence.

Jamelotti? She's calling me, the cunt. I didn't answer. I guess she's phoning to ask forgiveness. It's too late. Jamelotti, she must have the original papers on her. Don't forget. Has she called you?

Called to make a threat. She's going to call a press conference. I tried to placate her. I asked how much she wanted, to forget this whole thing. I offered her security, flights, she didn't accept. But she's fucked. Antonio José called. An informant gave a lead. She's staying at the Hilton Hotel. She thinks she's safer there. That we can't go in there. Now it's just a question of time. Her brother still hasn't managed to find her. Antonio José sent a detective, but he was with someone else, someone who goes by the book. That Gláucio guy who takes everything seriously. Incorruptible. We'll have to wait and see.

Call me. That'll make things better. Look, get them to break her face. Tell them to fuck her up. Burn every little bit with cigarettes. Burn that pussy of hers. Stick it up her arse. I want her to suffer. Motherfucker. Is it Silva who's going there? Good. Call me.

Wlamir sighed, relieved. He was nearing the end of this suffering. Did he want to know? No. It would only come to an end when he was certain he had all those original papers back.

Jamelotti, Silva must get hold of those papers. It's a matter of life or death, you know. Call me. This shit must end before the convention. How are we going to launch my bid for office in the middle of this mess? Ciao.

You must know, I'm not going to run away. I'm also not going to hand myself over. To be exposed to the sanctimoniousness of those bumbling idiots, honest and the like. Old enemies. Many people wanting to settle a score. All now with their tails between their legs, but give them half a chance and they'll bare their teeth. I'm not going to run away. If the shit comes I'll go to Castanhal. To the sawmill. I'll stay there for a while. Bugger that, I'm the governor of the state!

Fred and Pat. Pat ought to have arrived. He had woken with a fright. And she had come after him. That detective and the journalist knew where he was. He had to leave immediately. If he went to Pat, he would be tied down. But he would be safe with her entourage. Coward, he thought. The press would be with her. He could denounce him. But how, if he had no proof? He got dressed, picked up his laptop and went downstairs. Presidente Vargas was still covered in darkness. City Deli, across the road, was open. He went in to eat something. He felt that hand on his back, when he was at the counter. He turned round, frightened, cold in his stomach. It was the journalist. Did I frighten you? I don't know anything. Please, what happened to my family is just hitting me. But I know. I know everything. You need to know. Of course, if you wish, I won't tell you anything. Know what? Look, it's much more serious than you could have imagined. It would be best to go back to the hotel. To your room. Shall we?

Before crossing the street, Urubu stopped. There's someone waiting for you. You see that guy at the door there? I know him. He works directly with the chief of police. Antonio José. But I spoke yesterday with detective Gláucio Lima. It's best not to go back. They're loyal to the governor. You understand what I'm saying, don't you? Is there somewhere else? I was on my way to the Hilton. My girlfriend's arrived. Pat Harrison, the rock singer? Here in Belém? Yes. That's a surprise. I'm not much of a rock fan, but I know who she is. She's very famous. You think that's better? I do. Let's go.

At that time of the morning the only movement in the Hilton

lobby was pilots and cabin crew heading out. He went straight to the reception desk. Urubu remained downstairs. Fred went up. Martha opened the door, face swollen with sleep. Pat was sleeping on the sofa. He kissed her face. She woke up. Hugged him and kissed him intensely.

You shouldn't have come here. Well I came. Now I'm here, in your country, the Amazon, Brazil. The name of this city is Belém. Why did you leave so surreptitiously? Don't you like me any more? You left everything behind. I told you in my e-mail that I've got things I have to sort out. What things? What would keep you from coming back? I want to know. I love you, Fred. What is it that you can't share with me?

It's much worse than you could possibly think. It's dangerous. Very dangerous. Deadly serious, okay? You're very famous, have a lot to lose by being here. It's best that you go back.

Don't forget that I also had to fight to get to where I am. You can count on me, come on. Let's resolve this together. You can count on me. They killed my entire family. Murdered them. My father, my mother, the twins and Dondinha. Isabela escaped. But she's in hiding. I don't know where. I've been looking for her. It's an old story. I'm going to tell you and then you'll understand that you have to go back. Get out of here. I'll sort it all out and come back, I promise. There's some guy downstairs waiting for me. He's a journalist. He said he has all the evidence. It's just that we were at my hotel, nearby here, and the police were there. Don't even think about it. He said, and I agree, that everyone around here works for the governor. Yes, the governor of the state. It was him who ordered the killing of my family. Yes, the governor. I told you, it's a story that goes way back. To another city. Castanhal. My father had a sawmill. That guy, Wlamir Turvel, yes, Turvel, is involved in shady business. He took the sawmill, assaulted my father, raped my mother and made us flee that place. Cruelty. Pure cruelty. Ambition. Robbery. My father was left an invalid because of a kick in the spine. Injured his spinal cord. Isabela and I decided to take our revenge. But then I ended up in New York, met you. On Sunday night, it was already Monday morning, you were sleeping, I went to read my e-mails. Isabela had sent one saying that the governor had killed our whole family. That she needed help. What would you have had me do? Me there, with you, living a quiet life, comfortable, and my family here murdered, my sister hunted down. This governor has his fingers in all sorts of pies. He's in drug trafficking, illegal business with timber, extortion, everything you can possibly imagine. You see? Now do you realise the danger? And what can you, Pat Harrison, a successful rock star, do here in Belém, in Pará? Do you want to end your career? You have to go back. As soon as possible. Now you know why I was so secretive about Belém. About my family.

Pat, it's best if you go back. The record company aren't going to understand this. It could be the end of your career. You're worth a lot of money. It's his life. Let Fred sort out his problems and come back afterwards. You can have him fetched. Make use of the plane while it's here. We can go back now and Fred can follow later.

No. I'm staying. Martha, I know you're worried about me. Fred too. But I'm going to stay. I can't lose you. I'm staying. We can make the most of the international press that are coming here. Martha, call and find out when they're arriving. We'll make use of them to expose him. Isn't that what you want to do? Exposed, you might be able to arrange immunity for your sister. They won't have any courage. She'll appear. It'll come out in the newspaper. She'll find us. We can all go to New York. Isn't that what you want? It's dangerous, Pat, for the last time, go back to New York.

Second-lady. Sílvia quickly became known informally as the "second lady". She accompanied Turvel on his trips into the interior. Locked away in intimacy with the governor and in meetings with his team. For strangers she was merely a beautiful and perturbing consultant. On some weekends, she went with him to the house at the sawmill, in Castanhal. She knew very well where it was. She did not go to the warehouse. Said that she didn't like it. That it reminded her of the time when she was poor in Ananindeua. Gradually, that dry man, who only seemed interested in business, money, was opening his soul. He was affectionate, educated, gentle. She fulfilled his wishes. She was available, exclusively, when he wanted. Soon, apart from trips, she was called during the day, to the ministerial residence. At lunchtime. A car with tinted windows dropped her at a strategic entrance. Outside the door, red light, they said the governor was receiving someone important and could not be disturbed. Sometimes he spoke about politics. Of his re-election. He still needed some time in command of the state, before going off to Brasília. Do you know Rio de Janeiro? No? We're going tomorrow. I'll send for you.

In Rio. He gave her a wad of notes. Have a wander through the shopping mall. I've got things to sort out. We'll meet up later on. Do you want to go to the theatre? Okay. You choose.

She asked the driver to wait in the parking area. She went in one door, left by another. Called a taxi. Went to spend time on the beach. For the first time in a long time, she felt free to be Isabela, in a place where no-one knew her. Many would have loved to be in her position. Money in the pocket, her own driver, private jet, Rio de Janeiro. A mixed up life. Sometimes she felt it. No-one can pretend all the time.

But when she recalled her father, she remembered everything and her vengeance was reinvigorated. And it was close, very close. That trip was not just to be together, so that she could get to know Rio de Janeiro. It was to confirm details with a Colombian connection and the Rio traffickers. She heard him on the telephone, speaking in code, when she was getting dressed after making love. She saw the briefcase which he held on to. Everything was in there. Now, a little bit of luck and the circle would close. Almost completely. She had not yet managed to set the final trap. She was going to try. She had picked up the results of the last test when she had got back. Unsuspecting, he had left the cleaning of the large sofa on which they had had sex up to her. And also the condom which she, carefully, had picked up, tied, closing the end, and put it in her handbag. Earlier, she had pierced it with a needle. He had no children. That was his secret dream. Not with her of course. Child of a whore, he thought. But that was exactly part of the plan. To become pregnant. To blackmail. And when she was just about to give birth, to kill her own child. Yes, just like that. Painful? Criminal? Shocking? Unforgivable? Yes. All of those. She returned to the shopping mall. Bought something. The driver was sleeping. She knocked on the window. They went back. She came out of the bath. Turvel and Jamelotti in the room. Talking in low voices. Jamelotti looked at her. Turvel acknowledged her with a glance. She sat putting on her make-up. It was a consignment. A plane would land at a remote landing strip in Castanhal. One part would go to Rio de Janeiro, the other would be shipped to Surinam. Jamelotti was on his way out. She knew how he looked at her. Coward. He preferred the money to her. Nausea. Like a piece of merchandise. Knowing that everything was part of a plan made her smile. Darling, could you take off your clothes for me? Mimi... Please... It's the only thing I ask of you. That you stay naked, all the time, so that I can contemplate the true beauty that I have here, just for me. Will that make you happy? Happy? Very. More than anything. Ah, darling, just like that, what beauty, what beauty!

She had heard mention of Orlando Urubu for the first time one day, in his official residence. He had been there, requesting, once again, without success, an interview. Mimi was annoyed. Very. He said that just mentioning the name of that journalist gave him a rash. Rage. Frothing at the mouth. He still believes in investigative journalism. That's why he's poor and fucked. I just want to know who finances that Urubu newspaper, as it's called, to put the taxman on him and that's it. A good journalist is a bought journalist. Learn that, my dear. They're all dangerous. They like money. Blackmailers. Now that my re-election is coming, they want to do these deceitful interviews. Sorry, I'm annoyed, my dear. Ah, Mimi, forget about it. You've already got so much to worry about. A whole state to take care of! You should stop getting so hot under the collar and let your staff take care of him. You should relax a little, darling. Later on, I want my Mimi as strong as ever, powerful, just so, just so, you see that with me there's never this story of getting annoyed? At least he, Mimi dear, is very happy with me. That afternoon, Wlamir was in a greater hurry than usual. When she went to have a bath, he left saying he had to sort some things out in Jamelotti's office. Sílvia had the opportunity she had been waiting for. She took the camera out of her pocket and, her blood running cold, photographed Turvel's desk. She rearranged the papers. Picked up his briefcase, the famous briefcase with the receipts, documents, trafficking routes, everything. Finally she could execute her plan. Everything was in place. The test had been positive. She was pregnant. She developed the photos. Took copies. Caught a taxi. Went to Castanhal to find Netinho. He was the only person she could trust. She went to his house. Hugged his mother, who did not recognise her on principle, but told her that he was at OK Tyres. When she saw him, all her childhood flooded back and she could not hold back her tears when they embraced. It had been happy. She had played with Netinho. She had liked him. So she had thought. Alright, she had still been a child, but women grow up much faster. She saw in his eyes that she had chosen correctly. He still liked her. Who knows, when all this is over? What remains to be done? A kiss, and don't look back. Tears. She wiped them away. The time had come. At home, she said she would be spending a few days away. Mother was preoccupied, but said nothing. Dondinha looked at her strangely. Kisses for the twins. Hug for father. She held him tight. Bel, why such a tight hug? As if you're going on a long journey. My girl, you're going to miss the fireworks, my girl! And who's going to come with me and Dondinha on the pilgrimage?

She arrived at Fafá's apartment and asked to stay for a few days. She said nothing. She wrote the letter:

Wlamir Turvel, this is going to be the end of you. Now you are going to pay for all your crimes. Extortion, contraband, trafficking, blackmail, murder. You are going to pay. Do you remember one of your first crimes, in Castanhal? Do you remember the Pastri family? Do you remember that Sunday when you went with your goons to the sawmill, beat my father and left him unable to walk, raped my mother and evicted us from there? Do you remember? I remember. I am not Sílvia, your whore, your second-lady. I have always been Isabela Pastri. I made myself a whore to get my revenge. Now I'm going to the press and the whole world will know who you are. I am not going to the police because they have been paid off by you. I am going to find Orlando Urubu, the one who gives you a rash just at the mention of his name. He is going to slaughter you, my dear Mimi. You have also seen the results of the test. I am pregnant. For a long time I have been keeping your condoms and putting your sperm inside me. One day it had to work. Don't you really want a child? But it should not be the child of a whore, not so? How can it not be the son of a whore, being your child? Of course. I am pregnant and the whole world is going to know about it, firstly Cilene, of whom you are so scared. Your day has come, you prick, bastard, and I am happy. I am happy for my sacrifice. On that Sunday, at the sawmill, I vowed that I would get my revenge. That day has come. Isabela Pastri/Sílvia.

She called Pedro Bomba, the driver who always came to fetch her, and met him at Harbour Boulevard. She asked him to deliver it to Turvel. It's urgent. Tell him that it was me who sent it. I can't do it myself. Go, Pedro, please. Do this for me, won't you? A kiss, darling.

The remains of Friday and Saturday dragged on. She found the silence strange. Wlamir didn't call. The desire to call took hold. Sunday was drawing to an end. The firework display would start soon. She had never missed one. This would be the first time. She called her mother. The square was overcrowded. The sound was deafening. Sayonara was performing in the acoustic shell. Kisses. Her nervousness increased. Before midnight, she called again, to hear the benediction. The habit of someone who has lived almost their entire life there, alongside the Basílica. They were chatting. She heard the first fireworks. The family's cheering. The twins. Suddenly, her mother stopped talking. All she could hear was the sound of the fireworks. Fireworks? Shots? Screams? Groans? Shots? She screamed down the phone and no-one answered. The fireworks ended. The silence settled. The line was cut off. She called again. Engaged. The phone was off the hook. The sobbing burst out. Despair. Fafá, concerned. She couldn't manage to talk. Okay, I'll tell you everything. Should we go there? No. Not now. It could be worse. I must go now. Go where? I don't know. I shouldn't have come. I've been lying to you all along. Now I could be getting you into trouble. I must go. Don't go. I'm also angry with them. Now that I know everything, even more angry. No, girl, stay here. This is what you must do. Tomorrow I'll go there to find out, okay? You'll see it's just a problem with the phone, I know it, so many people around, some fireworks hit the phone box, you'll see it's nothing. Fred. He must be told. On the internet. E-mail. Man, they've killed everyone. Dad, mom, the twins and Dondinha. Come back and help me. It was him, Wlamir Turvel, because of our revenge. Come back!

Fafá left the house the next day, very confused. That was quite some revenge! What courage! Ah, if Carlito knew about it. Name changed, becoming the governor's lover and now this. She was divided between canine obedience to Carlito and the pure friendship that she felt for Sílvia. She was not used to Isabela. From the street, everything appeared normal. Windows open. She went to the doorman. She wanted to go up to the apartment of the Pastri family. He tried on the internal phone. No-one answered. There's no-one there. You'll see, they've gone out. Or they're sleeping after the festivities last night, the pilgrimage today. Sorry, I have orders not to let anyone go upstairs. I don't know of any problem with the telephones. Well, I have no telephone here. Try to call again. These phones are all haywire, really. They'll stop working all of a sudden and then come back on again. And you don't get anywhere by complaining. When the bill comes it's just bigger. She called Carlito who was not answering or was not getting a signal. Queens, these days, like artists, had their own special days.

Isabela called Turvel. He didn't answer. Son-of-a-bitch. He can see the number on his screen and isn't answering. Coward! She called numerous times. She called Jamelotti. Tell that murdering son-of-a-bitch that I'm going to completely fuck up his life. He killed my family! Coward! Mother-fucking drug dealer!

Silvinha, listen here. No. No, Silvinha, this won't get us anywhere. Which son-of-a-bitch has killed who? I don't understand anything. My girl, listen, you're very upset, okay? Where are you? Let's talk? We've always been friends, not so? Well then. You're very upset. Very nervous. I don't understand. Whose family is this? Yours? I don't know them. Well, as you know, he's a very busy man.

You know very well. Dear, let's get together and thrash this thing out. Then you can explain everything to me. I can guarantee you that when the Gov knows of it, he'll have everything sorted out. He'll get the police on it, everything possible. I'm very sorry, it really is a great pity.

Lying bastard, fat pig, son-of-a-bitch! You also know everything! You and he can go fuck yourselves! I'm going to call a press conference. I'm going to call all the newspapers. I promise you that! And tell your boss that it's best if he answers my phone calls! Silvinha, forget about this. Why such a fuss? Look, let's do this. You can be given some cash, a good sum, so that you can calm down. A million, okay? Go on holiday, let your hair down. Click!

Night arrived and nothing. Fafá had also not managed to talk to Carlito. Some or other getaway. That worm is out of range. Fafá, I'm not going to stay here. It's very dangerous for you. They can squeeze Carlito with some or other gossip, and you know that you're my dearest friend. They'll come knocking here and you could be in trouble. You could be eliminated. Go to a hotel. Go to the Hilton. The best of all. I'm going to hide out of sight from everyone. I'm going to talk to that Urubu. You want to know something? It would be good if you came with me. Now that I've got you into this, I can't just leave you here. Shall we? Take whatever you can, a few clothes, it's only for a couple of days. At reception, only I am going to give my real name, okay? To protect you. Me, no, I actually want to reveal myself.

In the room, she tried to call again. Now, not even Jamelotti answered. Night fell, and she went downstairs to go to the Alvino newsstand to pick up the Urubu newspaper and to call. Now it was coming to an end.

Who? Silva thought it worthwhile to conduct this service personally. He owed his meteoric rise in his military career to Turvel and Jamelotti. He was a colonel. Chief of police. A little longer, he would take his pension and that would be it. He would open his own security company. But going into the Hilton Hotel and killing someone was a bit too much. And now Sílvia, beautiful woman, whom he had always admired. And if something went wrong? Neither Turvel nor Jamelotti would come to his aid. They would tell another story. Run away. Deny any links. They're in charge, give orders and keep quiet. If this goes wrong, his life will be worth nothing. Everything will be over. He will be like a criminal, will be locked up, humiliating for his family, his children, so proud. And then, those two were no longer completely on top of things. The Colombians were worried. He called Favacho, old friend, to whom he went now and again for work of a very personal nature. Not even the Gov's people knew about him. It's important, man. Something personal, okay? But if you land in the shit I don't know who you are, okay? How much? That's it. I'm paying. You see? No debate. It's really important. Her name is Isabela Pastri. She's in room 702. We have an informant there, Silveirinha, who's working with the bellboy. He's going to wait for you in the garage, on the Olímpia side. He'll give you the key and get you there without anyone seeing. He'll wait for you. Make it over the top. Crush her. Beat her. I don't want any noise, but break her just the same. Go hard on her cunt, burn and cut her tits. I want it to seem like a crime of passion. And – most important – she's got some papers. They're with her. If it's not lying around there, look in her handbag, in the cupboards, just get those papers. They're documents and test results. No debate. Get them and bring them to me. I'll be waiting there on Trindade square. Are we on? I'm going to call Silveirinha. He's the little swarthy guy, dressed as a bellboy. He'll be there waiting.

Favacho went by the stairs. Waited a few seconds for two gringos who were waiting for the lift. They went up. He went to 702. Opened the door and came across a beautiful woman, in panties and a t-shirt. She got a fright, tried to run, but he grabbed her. He gave her a punch, full force, and she collapsed on the bed, her nose bleeding profusely. It's not me! It's not me! Three more hard blows to the breasts and the stomach. Where's the case? Where are the documents. I. Punch. Plea... Punch. There. He looked. Yes. Punch in the middle of the face. She fell unconscious. He held the pillow over her face. One, two, three, four, five shots to disfigure her. He took out his knife. Covered himself with a sheet. Cut off her nipples. Made a vertical slash down her stomach. Another cut much deeper. Inserted the knife into her vagina and turned it. Violently. And again. Just to make sure, he slit her throat. He picked up the documents. He wiped his gloves on a bath towel. His face to wipe off the sweat. He breathed deeply. He left the room. Silveirinha was waiting on the stairs. Silva was waiting on Trindade square. It's done. In the way I asked? Yes. Exactly. Beautiful woman, hey? She is. But now she was. She was meddling where she shouldn't have been. Here's part of the money. Tomorrow morning I'll give you the rest. To make sure there's no problems, you understand. The two of us. You and me. Of course. Thanks. Ciao. Doctor? It's Silva. It's done. They're with me. I'll bring them. Silva, it's confirmed? In the way I asked? It is. That's great. You're one of us. Wlamir? It's done. You can breathe easy. In the way you asked. Silva. He's bringing me everything. At once. He'll get the cash. Everything can continue as normal, thank God. Tomorrow, then, the convention and nomination? Yes, my lord. You're the boss.

Urubu. He went into the hotel suite with the envelope. In front of him, a beautiful American woman and Fred were waiting. There was also another woman, a secretary it seemed, who opened the door for him. Fred made the introductions and said that he would translate everything.

First, it's necessary for me to explain who I am and what I'm doing here. My name is Orlando Saraiva. The name Urubu was given by my enemies. I am a journalist in the fields of crime and politics. Through the years, I have been at all the newspapers and left because of a lack of independence. One discovers the facts, but can't publish them because the owner is put under pressure by the guilty parties. Because of this, I started publishing my own newspaper. Friends paid for the printing, as long as their names are not made known. They're also scared. I understand that. I have already received all types of financial propositions to shut me up and I have not accepted. I have faced a number of court cases and overcame them, one by one. I don't owe anything to anyone. Okay, I have a weak point. I'm married, not officially, with a woman, Edwina, who keeps a brothel, a meeting house. If she didn't know how to defend herself, having clients.so important that they prefer not to make things difficult, we would be in danger. I know her business is illegal, but I have only ever known her doing this and I've learnt to live with it. We don't live in the same house. Each to their own. That's how it is. What I am going to reveal to you is very serious. Fred ought to know part of the story, not all of it. This could cause a real revolution in the political scene here. Madam may not understand much, but Fred can explain. Excuse me, I know that you're famous because I'm a journalist, but I don't know your work. Actually, I listen mostly to Brazilian music, but when I have some free time, after all of this is over, I'm definitely going to listen to it. I would like to say that, personally, I don't know if madam should be running this risk, with the material we have here.

Orlando, Pat knows everything. I've explained to her. On the contrary, she wants to get involved. She's going to use her influence, with the arrival of the foreign press, even though they specialise in music, to divulge this.

Okay, that's great. You know, it will be very difficult to get any press coverage if you rely on the newspapers here. Those guys have probably hushed everything up already. Money, lots of money, for their silence. You must be curious as to how this arrived in my hands. By accident. Or perhaps for being known in this fight against crime. Someone, who it is not necessary to name, called me on Monday night. He didn't tell me where, he found a keyring and a key for one of the lockers at the bus terminus. He went there and found a bag with a change of clothing and this envelope. Inside, separately, a letter to a certain Netinho, asking him to hand this over to me. I'll explain it, you can read it. He saw all the other things, but he keeps to himself, he was nervous, called me and handed everything over to me. I went to meet him after I had bumped into you, Fred, at the vigil for your family. I was looking for her, but no-one knew anything. Strangely enough, a homosexual pimp, who might have been in contact with her, was murdered in a sauna, on Monday, but it's a fact that she had not been in contact with him for quite some time. It's obvious that, on reading, I realised that everything is aimed at nailing the suspects and the facts that the whole world knows about, but fear prevents from revealing. What we have here is explosive. It's going to end the political career of the governor of the state, Wlamir Turvel. Will put him in jail. You know that this afternoon is the party convention that is going to nominate him for re-election? Isabela calculated carefully, or was very lucky. I don't know if you know, but your sister got close to the governor as a call-girl, going by the pseudonym of Sílvia. In this way, I checked with a number of sources, she came to accompany the governor on trips to the interior and even to Rio de Janeiro. Imagine if it was revealed, just this and nothing more, that she had access to his office, completely unchecked. What I'm saying is here, in a copy of a letter that she sent to Turvel and attached to the documents. She explains what she did. Photographed documents, these here, which clearly show the involvement of the governor in contraband, drug trafficking, blackmail, illegal transport of timber, actually a whole host of crimes. But further, Wlamir never had children. She became pregnant by him, to make him suffer and guaranteed she would abort, only to have the pleasure of killing his child. Sorry, I know this is difficult, but it's all here, written down. Do you want to see the documents?

Where is she? I don't know. I'm like you, without a clue. Martha, set up a group interview for later on, still this morning. Good, Martha, that's alright, okay, at about four this afternoon. They've all arrived already. See if the local studio rep has managed to organise the local papers. Miss Pat... Please, just Pat. It would be interesting to arrange for the correspondents of newspapers from Rio de Janeiro and São Paulo. Very important. Martha, ask the guy who works here to arrange that with the studio headquarters here. It's best to say that I have huge revelations to make. Orlando, I think it would be good if you could stay here with us until the time for the interview. I believe we're all running a risk and now only Pat's fame is protecting us. Have lunch with us while we examine these papers more closely. I need to be up to speed with them by the time of the interview. Do you mind if I call home and let them know I won't be having lunch there? Orlando spoke on the phone and noted down a number. Isabela called. She left her name, but didn't leave a number. She'll call back later. This other number, bless him, is for Silveirinha, an informant who works here in the Hilton. He called and said he has something big. Can I call from here, now? Tell me, man, it's okay to speak. What big story is this that you've got for your friend? Don't come to me with gringo scandals. Murder at the Hilton? Okay, this is beginning to sound interesting. When? Have they discovered the body? Who was it? From here? From Pará? The name? Isabela Pastri… The body is here, still? Which room? The floor? Wait for me, I'm on my way. Sorry, Fred, I know this is awful, but you have to come with me.

Pat, you, no. Martha, don't let anyone in. Not even when the lunch comes, okay? Only when I come back.

Flight. Isabela came back in a carefree mood, making the most of the night breeze on Republic Square. She looked at the degeneration of Park Bar, today a prostitution den, and felt pity. But how could she feel pity when she herself was a prostitute, even if it was for a purpose that she believed was noble? She went up to room 702 and stood, petrified, on seeing the chaos. She held her hand to her mouth to contain the scream at seeing Fafá's bloody corpse. What to do first? If she holds her, she will also be covered in blood. She held her. Her face disfigured, obviously gunshots. The stab wounds. Such anger. Such violence. It wasn't just to kill, but to destroy the body. Her. It was supposed to be her. Fafá was in the wrong place at the wrong time. They had wanted to do this to her. Shaking, crying, she hunted around but could not find the envelope, which had been kept at the bottom of a handbag. He had done it, the motherfucker. Murderer. She fell to floor and cried. She couldn't think any more. She felt the force of all that violence. She doesn't know how much time has passed. She sighed deeply. She had to flee. The murderer could still be nearby. She had to call Orlando and reveal everything. Whatever might happen. The killer here did not know her. Must have passed on the news that she was dead. This could benefit her. My God, my friend, completely innocent, who led her life just as she wanted to. Yet another death on her shoulders, in the name of vengeance. Now, more than ever before, she had to kill Turvel. It was not merely vengeance. Now, justice would come with his death. She left the room and went out, at a loss. She wandered aimlessly and decided to sit at the hotdog cart next to the Olímpia cinema. If she at least knew where Luciano was. No. She couldn't bring anyone else into this. Killing more people. What to do? She went to the Iguatemi shopping mall. Visited all the floors. Went to the food hall. The smell of the food left her feeling nauseous. Fafá's body had not left her head. She heard announcements that the mall was about to close. She waited until the last moment. She waited outside, protected by the crowd which was waiting for the tram, guided by overhead cables into the middle of the street. She has nowhere she can go. She was all alone. She needed a computer. To send an e-mail to Fred. He should have arrived. Would he go looking for her at Fafá's house? Had he also been caught? Sending an e-mail might reveal her whereabouts. Confused, she can't think. She's scared of everything. She walks. She sits down on a bench in Trinidad Square. The church is closed. She slept there, curled up, in the open air. She woke up at the noise of a metal door slamming. Frightened, she saw a short, round man, dressed in a tracksuit, leaving a house. She decided to ask for help. Surprised, he was on the defensive, fearful of being mugged or being asked for money. She asked to use the bathroom. He let her. When she came out, he had a cup of coffee ready for her. He asked her what had happened. If she had been assaulted, mugged, if she lived in this street. Could he call the police? No. Not the police. Look, if I tell you, I could cause you problems. Can you run the risk, sir? Do you have a computer? The internet? No. The office where I work has it, but I've never needed it. She pulled out of her pocket that scrunched up newspaper. Do you have a phone? I need to call a journalist on this newspaper. Orlando Saraiva? I have his phone number. You do? Are you a friend of his? No. I had to look for it two days ago, I think. I had something I had to deliver to him. Here's his phone number. You can call. I'll wait.

Hello? Is that the residence of Orlando Saraiva? Is he there? No? Do you know if he might be coming back this morning? I'd like to leave a message. Tell him that Isabela Pastri called. I need to speak to him. It's urgent. I'll call back in one hour to find out if he has come back. Bye for now.

Isabela Pastri? Yes, why? I don't know what to say. This is all a huge coincidence. It's even sending a shiver down my spine. I'll explain. My name is Valdomiro Cardoso. I work in an accountant's office. On the eve of the Recírio, I was sitting at a little bar there on Generalissimo when I found a keyring. I've got a collection of keyrings. So I kept it. The next day I noticed that, among the keys, one of them was for a locker at the bus terminus. On weekends I'm a football referee. Sometimes, when I have to go some distance, I leave a change of kit in those lockers because I might have to come back and, quickly, go and ref at another match and don't have time to waste. I must confess that I committed an indiscretion. I went there and discovered a bag, which is here, I can show it to you, as I found it, but inside it there was also an envelope. I opened it and there was a letter addressed to some Netinho. Inside, another envelope, which was more bulky, I also read what was in it. I couldn't resist. You are very courageous, miss. Before you ask, I want to tell you that I handed it over to Orlando Saraiva. He already knows everything. Miss Isabela, I am a calm man, discreet, peace-loving. I was very scared when I read it. But even more so in meeting Orlando and handing it over. I asked him to forget my name. Never to mention me again. But what's most important is that he already knows. I think we can wait a little longer until he gets home. It might be soon. You know, these journalists have strange schedules. I don't know if you'd like to have a bath, I don't know, something? I live alone. I lived with my mother, in this house, until she passed away. I gave her clothes away, so I don't have anything to offer you. Perhaps a room to rest. Aren't you scared of helping me? I am. But I believe that all these coincidences are trying to tell me something. Who was this Netinho? A friend from Castanhal. A friend from childhood. There's no-one if I can't put my trust in him. I don't know what he was doing here, if it was him, who lost this keyring. It was God who sent you there, to the lockers. Thank you so much for handing the papers over. You could have thrown them away, out of fear. You might not have gone to fetch them. They would have stayed there until the administration came across them and then who knows.

Do you have the originals, miss? I had. They were stolen. I think it's all over. The copies are good enough for Orlando. He knows what to do with them. Where did you leave the originals? How were they stolen?

Do you really want to know? I hid at the house of a friend. I knew that they were hunting for me. Scared that they would find me, I went to hide in a very exposed place, to try and stop them. I checked in, with my friend, to the Hilton Hotel. Near here. I left to buy Orlando's newspaper and find his phone number. When I went back to the room, I found my friend murdered. All cut up. Shot in the face. I left there in a daze, like a mad person, walking about, I went to the shopping mall, scared of everyone and everything. I ended up sleeping outside here. I woke up with the noise of your door, this morning.

Miss Isabela, this is very serious. Let's wait for Orlando to come back. He'll know what to do. But until then stay here. They won't have any idea that you're here. Now, that's what's going to happen. You know that today is the convention for the governor? That convention is going to nominate him for re-election. It's today. Today? Yes, late this afternoon, I think. It ought to be in the newspapers. Zé must have thrown the newspaper on to the veranda. Give me a minute. Here it is.

Convention likely to nominate Turvel for re-election. The governor Wlamir Turvel is going to be nominated today by his party for re-election as governor of the state, at a convention which is to take place from five o'clock this afternoon, at the party headquarters. In the past few days, politicians from all the municipalities of Pará have been arriving for the event. Turvel has cancelled all his day-today appointments as governor so that he can dedicate himself to the political business at hand.

With Orlando Saraiva's help we are going to put a stop to that. He has to be exposed. It's going to be a huge scandal. I hope it will end his career.

Be careful. He is very powerful. People do anything for money, out of fear, out of loyalty.

I've got nothing to lose. I've already lost everything. Now, I live to see the end of him. I want to kill him. Listen, I know that there's nothing any more. I'm a calm person, you've seen that for yourself, miss. I get on with my life and don't want to hear about others. But perhaps this is the moment to let you know. You are very young still. Very beautiful. You've got your whole life in front of you. Isn't there too much scandal already? Isn't it better to get away from here, travel, go far away, start a new life somewhere else? From what I read, you're pregnant, aren't you? Well, you have this child who could change your life. Put that revenge aside. No. I also thought about that, but, Mr Cardoso, I took a vow. My life has been devoted to this vengeance. Turvel did not finish my family off when he murdered them. He finished them a long time ago when he assaulted my father, my mother and my brothers. I am going to finish this thing, even if I have to go to that convention by myself. Even if I have to kill him. I'll go to prison. My life has already ended, but his also has to end. If you'll excuse me, I'd like to call again.

Saraiva had not returned. Gradually, the silence was growing between the two of them. When he looked up, he saw that Isabela was asleep. Valdomiro left her. First he had admired that woman, so beautiful, so courageous and so determined. He should not expect everyone to be like him. Why can't he make her see reason? How can he prevent her from doing all that? He felt sorry, wanted to help, to protect. That striking woman in his house, so vulnerable. With someone like that, he might even think of sharing his life. If she could just look at me one day. Valdomiro, stop being such an animal. She is a beautiful woman, accustomed to a life of luxury. Look at yourself, ugly, fat, balding. You cripple. He left her sleeping. He called Orlando Saraiva himself. He called the office. He was sick. Couldn't come to work. In days gone by, felt it was his duty, he was rarely absent. Okay.

702. There were men from the special service of the military police in the room, collecting fingerprints. The body had been covered with a sheet. Fred Pastri's entire life had passed in front of his eyes when he and Orlando had gone down in the lift to the seventh floor and gone to room 702. Dazed, he had gone in behind Orlando.

So, Urubu. Have you got your feelers out, hey? Damn, man, the body is still warm and you're already here? Shit!

Is it a woman? What's her name? A gringa? Is she from around here? Isabela Pastri? Never heard the name, he pretended. Murdered? Let me see?

Urubu lifted the sheet. He was used to such scenes. Even so, he was taken aback. He closed his eyes. He went back to Fred and whispered. Look, it's heavy stuff. The face is really disfigured. Calm down. He is with me, personally. My deputy. I'm getting old. That okay? Fred took a look. Froze. For two reasons. Firstly because of the horrible vision of that face torn apart by a number of shots. Secondly because, even in that condition, he knew that he was not looking at Isabela. He would recognise the face of his sister, no matter what. He trembled, tears came to his eyes, he swallowed. He whispered to Orlando. It's not her. I know. I know my sister. Are you absolutely certain? I am. Good show. But I think its best to let them think what they want. We can gain some time. Good idea. More confidently, without fear of shocking Fred, Orlando lifted the sheet to see the other wounds. Damn, the guy who did this was an animal. Damn, it wasn't enough to shoot her, he had to use a knife as well! This woman must have made him really angry. This here is the result of passion. Look, that's the only way he could cut her breasts! And her pussy, shit! What's that for? Pitico, you'll let me see, once they're done, the results of the tests? Yeah. I'll call you. Okay. I'm going to check other details at reception. I've already got those. Look here. Did you see what time she arrived? No-one saw this man or this woman coming in. You know how it is, luxury hotel, discretion and such shit. The manager is completely pissed off with us. They want the body out of here. He's even been up here already to try and keep the hotel from getting involved in the scandal. For my part, I'd also like to get going soon, but I have to fill in all this shit. Have a cold one for me, okay, my friend? I'll call. Ciao. They left. Talking can wait until they're upstairs.

Darling, you have to go back. He sat down and cried. What happened? Your sister? The press has already been informed. Calm down! Calm down! Shut up, dammit! Sorry. Sorry, Pat, you don't understand what I'm saying. Pat, it wasn't my sister. I don't know what happened. According to the hotel, she was in that room with a friend. If that's not her body, then Isabela is alive, I think. Where, I don't know. They cut up the body. Shot her in the face. Darling, you don't have to stay here. Your career... Fred, enough, okay? I'm going to call Silveirinha. He'll shed some light on this story.

Silveirinha? Shit, man, you want me to go publishing untruths... Yes, I was there. No it's not Isabela Pastri. No it isn't. I'm certain. Look, I'm here with her brother. Her own brother. How more certain can you be? Now, that's enough. If she was in the Hilton, where is she? Wrong room, she was in another one, went out, what time, gone, give me the whole story, man. I'm here. In the Hilton. In the presidential suite. Yes, with the American rock star. That's enough, man.

Now, we must get organised. We must look at those documents, one by one, sort them out so we can explain it at the press conference. Fred, get a grip. We're going to need you in control of yourself.

Mr Antonio José? It's Silveira, here at the Hilton. Sorry to call you like this, but it's urgent. The girl they killed, it's not Isabela Pastri. It wasn't Isabela Pastri that they killed. I don't know. I'm going to check the register. She was with a friend. You'll see, she escaped. I don't know. Orlando Urubu. Yes. He's here. He said he's with the girl's brother and he saw the body. This brother is with an American singer in the presidential suite. Some Pat something or other. It wasn't Silva, no. Someone else. I've never seen him before. Yes, sir. I met him, escorted him to the room and took him to the exit again. No-one saw. I don't know, sir, I'm going to investigate and if there's something I'll call. Look, I don't know if you're interested, but there's going to be an interview with this singer and the press now, at about four this afternoon. It's full of gringo journalists at this hotel. Positive.

Martha, call Mr Wilford, my lawyer. Now. Wilford, how's it going? I'm in Brazil. I need to make use of your services. My boyfriend is Brazilian. Fred Pastri. He is being threatened by drug dealers. Nothing. He has nothing to do with drugs. It's a local thing. But a huge thing. The governor of the state is involved. Wilford, with all due respect, I didn't ask for your opinion. No. It's a problem of my own. I know what I'm doing. That's why I called you. Speak to the authorities. With that anti-drug squad. With the embassy. I want safe passage for him. You know, political asylum, something like that. I need protection, here. I don't know if we can trust in the local police. I don't think so. Do it now. Martha will give you the details. Speak later.

Ladies and gentlemen, Pat Harrison. The hall at the Hilton Hotel was full of recorders, laptops, cameras. Apart from the international journalists, there were correspondents from Rio de Janeiro and São Paulo, and reporters from the local cultural magazines, all with CDs to autograph.

Good afternoon. It is a great pleasure to be here in Brazil, for the first time. I came to discover the Amazon and have been overwhelmed by the little I have seen, between the airport and here. So green, beautiful trees, a most appealing city. It's obvious that there's a great deal of poverty as well, but I think that this is a global problem, or almost global.

Pat, are you going to record something here in Brazil or will your new music reflect the influences of this trip? Nick, thanks for the question, but this press conference, actually, is for another matter. I know that the publications and media organisations that came here expected to hear about matters relating to my music and the like. But today is going to be different, nevertheless I do believe you will all leave much more satisfied. The purpose of this press conference is an exposé. A most serious revelation. It will be carried in the pages of all the newspapers of the world, but principally in Brazil.

An exposé that will leave you shocked, but will have you running to transmit it on the internet, even offering it to the big news organisations of the United States and England. One moment, ladies and gentlemen, I would like to call on Fred Pastri, my boyfriend, Brazilian, from here in Pará, and the journalist Orlando Saraiva, also from here in Pará.

Ladies and gentlemen, good afternoon.

One by one, the documents were shown and commented on, analysed, explained. The conference lasted almost two hours, with exclusives for a number of broadcasters. Finally, Pat took up the microphone and thanked everybody. Thank you for coming here. Thank you for broadcasting. For exposing to the world this mafioso who is guilty of a number of crimes. I have already asked for protection from my embassy. Safe passage for Fred. I did not ask it for Orlando, nor did he want it. It's his life. The path he has chosen. I would also like to inform you all that last night, in this hotel, a woman was mistakenly murdered. Who should have been killed was Isabela Pastri, Fred's sister. She escaped, but we don't know where she is hiding. If, after this news is out, she appears, please let us know. The press conference is over. We will be in our suite, waiting to see what happens. You, ladies and gentlemen, have been informed of everything. I'm sorry I didn't give you any news about my music, but I trust that you are satisfied.

Bugger. Wlamir, she escaped. How did she escape? I don't know. Antonio José called me. The informant told him. Another woman was killed. I sent Silva, dammit. Silva knows her very well, how did he make that mistake? I'm going to get that son-of-a-bitch. He's going to be fucked. Don't you worry. Dammit, Wlamir, Silva is our man, you know that. If he made a mistake, I don't know. But look, this thing is fucked up. That son-of-a-bitch Urubu. It's happening now. There's a general press conference with that gringa singer. Of course. Sílvia's brother, Urubu and the singer are denouncing us. They're showing proof. They have a copy of the material. I don't know. The originals came with Silva. Motherfucker. It's going to collapse. I'm not going to any bloody convention. I'm not going to stare at the contempt of those shits, anxious to screw me. You and Miso can represent me. Go, bugger it. I'm going to Castanhal. I'll stay there. No-one will get me out of there. I'll be waiting. Call Antonio José. Throw the shit in the fan. Have him kill that singer, the boyfriend, Urubu, bugger it! Gone to shit. Don't you think so? It's us or them. Then this thing will get sorted. Fuck it. Call the newspapers. Speak to the bosses. Silence, you hear? I don't want anything published. Now I want to see if they respect the money they received. They like the kickbacks. Now I want to see.

Jamelotti was watching the TV. Breaking news. Breaking news. Governor of Pará exposed as the head of a criminal network involved in numerous illegal activities. The governor Wlamir Turvel was exposed today at a press conference at the Hilton Hotel by Fred Pastri and the journalist Orlando Saraiva…

You see? Motherfuckers! Vultures! I'm going, Jamelotti. This is not the end of it. We've got the judges. They got guts. But have them killed.

Knocking at the door. Come in! It was Silva. Are you crazy, hmm, dammit? That woman is still alive! Very much alive! Why didn't you go yourself, dammit! The man already knows. He's pissed off with you. Me too. Are you blind, hmm, dammit? Can't you do anything right? Now that you're well off you just want to sit on your arse? Son-of-a-bitch, Silva. Dammit, it's incompetent. Killing the wrong woman, shit. You got the envelope. At least the envelope, hey? You have it, dammit. Where is it? What is it? Are you just going to stand there, staring at me like a zombie. Let's get moving, I don't have time to waste, dammit. What is it?

Sorry, boss. Nothing personal. Just business. Silva pulled a nylon rope out of his pocket and, quickly, wrapped it around Jamelotti's neck. Too fat, he couldn't react. He fell on to the chair. Stamped his feet. His face, red, was about to explode. Silva kept pulling as hard as he could. He saw the rope cutting into the fat skin and bleeding. He stopped when there was no further reaction and Jamelotti's face was blue.

Now. Isabela woke with a start, sweating. It took her a few seconds to remember where she was. She recognised the place. Headache. She had slept heavily, dreamless. She looked around. The man's house was meticulously tidy. Where was he? Mr Valdomiro? Excuse me, Mr Valdomiro? He wasn't there. She went to the toilet. Wandered into his room. So many movies. As she went out, she had the idea of looking for a gun. With so many alarms on the house, he ought to have a gun. She went to the most obvious place, the bed-side table and searched through it. It was loaded. Wlamir also went around armed. He had showed it to her. She knew how to handle it. She put it in her handbag. It would be best to go straight to the convention. A noise. Fear. She held the gun. Had she been found out? Relax. You're safe. Do you remember me? Valdomiro Cardoso. You're in my house. You fell asleep exhausted. Everything's okay. I went out to buy some chicken so we could eat. What time is it? Almost three in the afternoon. Already? My God, I have to… Relax. Don't you want to eat, have a bath? There's no time. I have to… Isabela, there's still time to reconsider. There is suffering, but not even for that should we go backwards. You're so young, beautiful, intelligent, stop doing this. Where are you going? Eat something. You might not feel like it, but if you don't eat, you won't have any strength. Let's go. Wait a few minutes. Eat something and I'll go with you. No. You must stay here. At home. Where you belong. Peaceful. Living. Me, no. I'm going. Perhaps I've spent my entire life following orders, doing everything not to be noticed. Now could be my hour. Do as you please. You already know what you're letting yourself in for. I want to give my help. I stayed watching you sleeping. I know that it shows a lack of sophistication, but I stayed, I must confess. Don't be offended, but you are very beautiful. I'm attracted to you. Don't be offended, I know very well what I am. But it's just that… It's time. Let's go.

They had asked the taxi to park a few metres from that old house, the party headquarters, on Governor José Malcher Street. They were waiting. There was much movement. Drumming. Fireworks. Time dragged on. Almost five. The driver, who had been chatting with his colleagues, came back saying they said on the radio that the governor's not coming. Had to go on a trip. Haven't you heard about the revelations? Now, this afternoon. There was even a special programme on the TV. Big shit. Some American rock singer and her boyfriend together with that journalist, Urubu, accused the governor of running a drug ring and other stuff. They showed the proof and everything. I think that's the reason. Are you going to stay here, then? Saulo Miso got out of an official car. He ignored the press. Went straight into the headquarters. Wait here. Isabela saw Pedro Bomba parking the car and getting out to go and chat with the other drivers. He saw her. Waved. Came up to her. Where've you been, girl. Have you heard about the shit? Only just. Where's Mimi? He didn't come here. Also, after this mess, you'll see. I know. Where's he gone? Miss Sílvia, I'm not authorised. You know, miss. Pedro, please, Mimi needs help right now. You know that he likes me. He needs help. Alright, miss Sílvia. He went to Castanhal. To the sawmill. To the house at the sawmill? That's it. Are you going there, miss? I am. Please don't tell anyone. Don't worry. I don't have anyone to tell. As she was leaving, she saw Colonel Silva nearby. She quickened her pace. She didn't like him. He was known as an assassin. She called the taxi driver. We're going to Castanhal. In a hurry. You can stay here if you wish, Mr Cardoso. I'm going.

Pursuit. Pat and Fred, this is just too much. It's time to go back home. This is all such a mess. The people at the record company are worried. Your lawyer called. The embassy as well. Don't you think you've made enough of a mess? Martha, shut up, okay? Sorry, I also think its dangerous, but okay. The doorbell rang. The local representative of the record company told them it was detective Walter Carmim of the federal police. Let him in. No, wait. Is the chap from the consulate here? He is. Let him in as well. The two of them together.

Good afternoon everyone. I am detective Walter Carmim, federal police. It's in regard to the revelations made by you, a short while ago. I received orders from Brasília to collect the proof you presented and also to question you as to how it came to be in your possession. The man from the consulate said immediately that Pat was an American citizen and was not to be questioned. Okay, that's a matter of jurisdiction, but if there's information she might be willing to hand it over. And you, Mr Pastri? I'll tell you. I have nothing to hide. I live in the United States. I received an e-mail from my sister, asking for help. When I arrived, I found out about the murder of my entire family. You might have heard about that, sir. My girlfriend, Pat, also came to Brazil. We met up here at the Hilton, and this journalist, Orlando Saraiva, then came to us with all this evidence. The next thing, we heard about the murder, in this hotel, of my sister. I expect you have also learnt of this. We set up a press conference and made the revelations. For my part, that's it.

And you, Orlando. I had access to these documents. I knew about the arrival of Fred, who didn't know of their existence, and I showed it to him. We decided to call a press conference to make the denunciation. Of course, you know the law, as a journalist I am not obliged to reveal my sources. That's true, I know. But I would like to have the documents. No problem. We'll have copies made. Fred, could you ask Martha? Yes. Here they are.

One more thing. Do you plan on going anywhere? I would like to be informed. It's for your protection... I understand. See you later.

Okay, I need to know where my sister is. The medical examiner, someone, is going to realise that it wasn't her who was killed.

The embassy is going to send someone here, for protection, but they're only going to arrive much later, at night, after ten. I think it's best to wait, it'll be safer that way.

Look, the governor must have arrived at the convention. You know, the convention that's going to nominate him for re-election. He probably already knows about the exposé and I doubt he'll go. Let me make a few phone calls.

It's like this. Jamelotti, who was chief of staff, doesn't answer. At the residence, the governor's not there. I spoke with the housekeepers there and at his house. The one at his house told me that the governor didn't go to the convention. He went to Castanhal. He has some sort of hideaway there, in a house with a sawmill alongside. Sawmill? Castanhal? That was my father's. Son-of-a-bitch. Sorry. You want to find your sister? I have a hunch. Wherever the governor goes, she'll be there. Want to take a bet? Let's get going. Is the car downstairs? Let's go through the garage. We can all go together. Are we going? Come on. No, Pat, you're not going. Neither am I. I'm a coward. I'm scared. My God, what a coward I am! I've got no courage. She always wanted to get revenge more than I did. I just wanted to get on with my life. Orlando, you can go. I'm not going. Martha, can we go to the plane? Hey, finally someone said something sensible. Let's go. Fred, you're not coming? You sure? I am. It's too much for me. It's too much. I'm a coward, for the love of God! Orlando, call this number. It's local. I hired one. Let me know of anything.

The return. The afternoon was still bright although it was almost seven in the evening when they arrived at Castanhal. Now where to, miss? There'll be a sign. There it is. Go in on the left. All the way down. Good road, huh? Tar like a carpet. What's it for, miss? The governor had it done so he could get to his sawmill in comfort. Even so, he prefers to come by helicopter. Only for the selected few. There, there, go that way. On that narrow dirt track? That's it. Isabela knew that she could not go through an entrance where she would be recognised. Too risky. They went in on a very tortuous road, potholed, full of obstacles, by which, eventually, there was a hut, next to the river. At the top of a steep bank. Could you wait here please? You're going back, miss? I'm going back. You can wait.

She knocked on the narrow door. Opened it. In the depths, an elderly man was lying down under a mosquito net. Uncle Haroldão! Haroldão! Who's that? Isabela. Do you remember me? Belzinha, as you used to call me. Girl, come closer to the lamp so that I can see you properly. My eyes aren't what they used to be.

Girl, of course, Belzinha, how long it's been! What memories! Could you believe that this girl, a little child, wandered all around here as a kid, as a picaninny! And now look at this grown woman, hey... Ah, my girl. Have you come on a visit? Do you need anything? Uncle, do you still have that pôpôpô? I do. Not the same one, another one, which is also very old, like its owner, but it works well. Great. What do you want with a boat, at this hour? It's dark. I need a favour. I need to borrow it. I want to get to the house, along the river. But it's dangerous. The tide is up. It's dark. That's now the house of the governor. He's got guards all around him. Why don't you just go along the road? Uncle, I need the boat. Is it something dangerous? Does he know you're going there? Look, don't go getting into any trouble. You're a very beautiful girl. Who is that man with you? A friend. A close friend. He's coming with me. Coming to look after me. Okay. My girl, how's it going with my old friend Fred? And your mother? Damn, it's been a long time. They... they're doing well. Give them a hug for me. There's something that you're not telling me. You know, my girl, when one gets old, you get to reflect a lot about life. Here, in this peaceful setting, I think a great deal. I stay here, peacefully, fishing, with this beautiful view. This here is a paradise! Why would I want to take myself off to the city, with all that stress, all that rushing to get nowhere, hm? I say that because I think that you are stressed. I'm scared. For you. Okay. You can go. But when you come back, stop by here to chat a little longer. So that we can recall some of those good times. My God, how you've grown into a beautiful thing, Belzinha. Look, can I come with the two of you? No. Please, Haroldão, it's just the two of us going. We'll come back quickly to chat, okay? Kisses.

Look at that rain! Mind you don't catch a cold. See you in a while! She turned the boat in the right direction, started the motor and went. Isabela felt herself going back to being surrounded by a happy time. The landscape. The air. The smell of the river. Smell of damp forest. Feeling the rain beating on her face. She wished she had never left that place. Had never grown up. Haroldão made sense. This was paradise! When she caught sight of the boathouse, the longing disappeared. It was now. There were no guards. Perhaps because of the rain. Completely empty. Deserted. Silently.

She tied the boat and they went up. They kept to the shadows of the trees. They got close to the house and saw him. Wlamir Turvel on the telephone, sitting on the sofa in the library. Before Valdomiro realised it, Isabela already had the revolver in her hand. Sorry. I found it at your house. It might be necessary. If you want, stay here. I'm going inside. I'm going as well. There's a side door. Few know about it. Come.

Wlamir looked surprised when he saw them. He hung up the phone. So, Sílvia isn't Sílvia after all. Sílvia is Isabela Pastri. You know, I should have killed you all on that day, in this very place. Pity. I had a soft heart. Now I'm paying for that. I was expecting you, actually. You pulled a fast one on me. Pulled a fast one on old Turvel. Mimi. Imagine that, someone calling me Mimi. And I let you. You deceived me. I liked you. I told you many times. I think I'm getting old. I liked you as a woman. A whore in bed. You did it all. And a good lay. I opened doors for you, you cunt. You mother-fucker. You whore. I opened the doors of my life. You used your pussy to deceive me. I loved you, Sílvia. I love you. I've never been in love before. And now you're pregnant with my first child. I read it, part of your revenge. But he is not the son of a whore. Not to me. He is my child and from the woman I love. It's always been busi-ness. Always been like that. I fucked the girls and ciao. I came to like you, and you did this to me. But this is the end of it. There's always time to do what is necessary. Your family is dead. You should already be dead, as well, but the documents you pho-tographed are back with me. With Jamelotti. He called me. This is the end of it. Your brother exposed everything. This is the end of it. I'm the governor. I can't go to jail. To get me out of my position, you'll need a lot more than that, and I'll pay off the whole world. They're already bought. Politicians, the press, everyone. This here is Brazil. This is Pará. From love to hate in one step, you know that. I hate you, but, thinking about it, I love you, Sílvia. I was here, thinking. Listen, who is this fat little man next to you? He's my friend. He came with me. And that gun in your hand? Is that for me? It is. You? You're going to shoot me? I doubt it. It's not in your nature. You faked it well just for the sake of betraying me. Were you faking? Those times, in bed, when you were in ecstasy, was it all fake? I looked into your eyes and saw love. That's why I believed. You were faking it?

I faked it. Do you want to know where I found the strength to face up to you? You know. On that day when you beat my father and raped my mother, on that day I changed. Changed for the rest of my life. Every time I was about to break down, I just reminded myself of that scene to regain my strength. I faked it. This baby, I'm going to have the courage to abort it. I'm going to kill it as well. I know it's an evil thing to do, but it's evil against evil. Now your time has come. You've been exposed on TV, on the radio and this morning in the papers. That will end your farce, Turvel. Turvel? Don't you call me Mimi any more? Sílvia, I'm the same man I've always been, with just one difference. I love you. I say that without any fear, because that way it makes me feel better. I love you. Go back. These revelations won't lead to anything. But I forgive you. I forgive you because I love you. Let's live together. Us and our little baby. I'll sort it out with Cilene and there we go. We can get on with our lives. I'm actually also getting tired of all this nonsense. Power, I've got. Money, too. I don't give a damn about power. I won't try for re-election. And then we can travel, plant roses, be in love, be in love, bring up our child, live our life. How about it? What do you think?

I don't believe a word you say. I don't love you. I hate you with all my being. I have devoted my life to this revenge. I will only be happy when I have ended your life. I have the gun and I am going to shoot. Shoot you and be happy. Look, Sílvia, now I also have a gun. I can also shoot, not so? But I don't want to. Put yours down as well. You love me, don't you? Don't you love me? I wanted to fake it. Every day when I got home I thought about what I had done. Each time I was with you I was filled with anger at what happened. You, yes you, bastard, who I should kill. To revenge my family. Yes you, I came to love. I love you. I don't want to kill you. I don't want to kill my child. I want to be happy, but with you. Please, put down the gun. Let's talk. I always thought that you loved me. No-one fakes it that well. It was in your eyes, no matter how much despair you felt. I am certain that your friend will understand me. Can't we talk? We have a child. We have our bond. Come, put down the gun.

The shot hit Turvel in the side. She shot first. He fell. Isabela, rooted to the spot. I don't love you, bastard. I hate you. The shot was well-aimed, to the chest. She fell, groaning. Valdomiro, took two shots in the head and fell into a chair. Wlamir picked himself up and dragged himself over to her. He embraced her. Damn whore, he whispered. He put the final shot into the back of her head. He heard the door creak. Silva, damn, what shit is this, hmm? Hey? Ah, okay, everything is alright. Understood. Is that really necessary? I don't believe it. Jamelotti isn't answering. Was it Ramirez who sent you? Was it? Answer, son-of-a-bitch! It was. Sorry nothing personal, it's just business. They fired. Wlamir was hit in the head. Silva in the chest. He lay in agony for a few minutes. With a final effort he tried to get up. A final gush of blood and he died.

A van drove up. Orlando Urubu. Fred, Pat and Martha at the airport. Martha answered the phone. Passed it over to Fred. He just listened. Hung up. All dead. My sister. The governor. Orlando is there. It's going to be a big scandal. He curled up. Like a foetus. He wept. The man from the consulate went to sort out the travel arrangements. He came back with an American gentleman, an official from the American embassy in Brasília. There's been a shooting in Castanhal. The governor and three other people have been killed. It would be best if you left right now. Please, Miss Harrison. There is no time to be wasted. It has to be right now. The little jet taxied and lifted off from Val de Cans international airport. Among the passengers, deathly silence.